PENGUIN MODERN CLASSICS

The Princess of 72nd Street

ELAINE KRAF (1936–2013) was a writer and painter. She was the author of four published works of fiction: *I Am Clarence* (1969), *The House of Madelaine* (1971), *Find Him!* (1977) and *The Princess of 72nd Street* (1979) – as well as several unpublished novels, plays and poetry collections. She was the recipient of two National Endowment for the Arts awards, a 1971 fellowship at the Broad Loaf Writers' Conference, and a 1977 residency at Yaddo. She was born and lived in New York City.

ELAINE KRAF

The Princess of 72nd Street

With an Introduction by Melissa Broder

PENGUIN BOOKS

PENGUIN CLASSICS

UK | USA | Canada | Ireland | Australia
India | New Zealand | South Africa

Penguin Books is part of the Penguin Random House group of companies whose addresses can be found at global.penguinrandomhouse.com

Penguin Books (PMJ), Penguin Random House UK,
One Embassy Gardens, 8 Viaduct Gardens, London SW11 7BW

penguin.co.uk
global.penguinrandomhouse.com

Penguin Random House UK

First published by New Directions Publishing Corporation 1979
Published with an Introduction by The Modern Library, an imprint of Random House 2024
First published in Penguin Classics 2024
003

Printed and bound in Great Britain by Clays Ltd, Elcograf S.p.A.

The authorized representative in the EEA is Penguin Random House Ireland, Morrison Chambers, 32 Nassau Street, Dublin D02 YH68

A CIP catalogue record for this book is available from the British Library

ISBN: 978–0–241–71527–7

Penguin Random House is committed to a sustainable future for our business, our readers and our planet. This book is made from Forest Stewardship Council® certified paper.

MIX
Paper | Supporting responsible forestry
FSC® C018179

For Kay Burford

INTRODUCTION

MELISSA BRODER

The Princess of 72nd Street, first published by New Directions in 1979 when Elaine Kraf was forty-three, is an avant-garde tale of one woman's seventh manic episode—a period of euphoria and hallucination, which she calls her "radiance"—and her desire to love from there, write from there, and perhaps, least tenably, live from there.

Ellen is a portrait painter who, as "Princess Esmeralda," rules the land of 72nd Street on the Upper West Side of Manhattan in the 1970s. When she isn't being checked into Bellevue, Roosevelt Hospital, or St. Vincent's to be treated with Thorazine and Stelazine, she governs her fiefdom of filmmakers, watermelon salesmen, musicians, shopkeepers, bartenders, and bricklayers by watching over them, sleeping with them, and occasionally, dancing topless with them.

The Princess of 72nd Street asks progressive questions about personal freedom, mental conditions, and self-governance. Who is entitled to hold power over the inner world of another? What defines sanity? Must a functional society be rooted in consensual reality? The novel also explores the question of how much happiness we are allowed as individuals, and the line between mania and a state of spiritual grace. While Kraf does not always provide clear answers to these questions (the human psyche is a nebulous realm, and this is literature—not a textbook—after all), the novel's inquiry is ahead of its time.

Apart from perpetrating a Robin Hood–like theft from a local market (she steals goods and then distributes them to her "subjects"), Ellen doesn't appear to cause any harm to others during her radiances. She is eccentric, dressing in costumes that have her taken for "a hooker, Sabra, American Indian, actress, ballerina, witch, holy saint, mother, girl, mystic, ethereal spirit, bitch, earth goddess, and more." A revolving door of men enter and exit her bed, including an Argentinian pianist, an attorney, an illusionist, a friend's husband, a doctor, and a vine-like man who smells of spices (not to mention an artist ex-husband and an academic boyfriend who came before them). For the Princess of 72nd Street, the "bubbles" and "feathers" and "white moths" of radiances are meant to be shared, not kept to oneself. She longs to share her joy with society, but society is not ready for this level of liberation—carnal, material, or otherwise.

"People like to pretend that radiance is something else when they see it," says the Princess, who describes the injections that terminate her episodes as the doctors' attempts to "make me stop bothering everyone with my happiness." The characters in Ellen's orbit believe that it is their right and responsibility to constrain these periods of mania—beatific experiences where "orange flowers" grow from her body and joy cracks out of every "pore or petal or cell." Yet, *is* it their right?

Complicating this question is the fact that none of the auxiliary male characters in the novel are particularly sane themselves. There is Auriel, an illusionist who fakes his suicide. There's Peter, the painter who has an emotional allergy to plums (the result of his girlfriend's obsession with using them as the subject for her own paintings). Ex-husband Adolphe is ravenous for success and has nervous breakdowns when his work involving a traffic light appears to be not only copied but improved upon. Ex-boyfriend George prohibits laughter and singing, and rips rags and foams at the mouth when challenged. In spite of their own madness, they single out Ellen as the insane one.

Such ambiguity is underscored by George's psychiatrist, Doctor

Clufftrain, who is the least sane character of all. Clufftrain sees patients around the clock from six A.M. until three A.M. He trembles, fears heights, and has no boundaries between himself and his patients. He instructs them to run his errands and treats them as his alter egos. He prescribes Ellen a mysterious drug that causes her to faint and throw up. It is unsurprising, then, when the doctor ultimately has a full psychotic break, a turn of events that articulates the question: Who is really an expert on mental health? Is the Princess experiencing illness when in her radiance? When the authority is sicker than his patient, her diagnosis may be seen as a sane reaction to an ailing society.

And yet, despite Ellen's desire to stay in a state of radiance eternally (who wouldn't want to stay in that ecstatic realm where the body is "light as a flower" and one's hair seems to "fly up and outward like wispy silk"), the Princess must concede that her beloved state is unsustainable.

As Ellen is about to enter radiance seven, she writes herself notes like DON'T LET STRANGE MEN INTO YOUR APARTMENT and MONEY IS THE MEANS OF BARTER in order to preclude behaviors that could get her hospitalized again. She feels an unsafe lack of pain during periods of peak radiance, and awakens with black-and-blue marks, scratches, and a lump on her head. She acknowledges the dissonance created by her promiscuity during radiance and her belief in monogamy. She finds the spiritual ranting of her cherished illusionist Auriel—the only person to whom she has revealed her princess status—boring. As Ellen, she longs for a pedestrian husband with money. And, while she resists the desolation that follows her radiance, longing for her fear to be turned into "mist" and for the return of "doves" and to be part of "the vision of stars" and to remain "a child forever," Ellen ultimately chooses to ground herself on Earth.

Whether she is the Princess, full of radiance and flooded with a feeling of "small bells ringing and showers of light," or simply Ellen, dropped into the pit of depression, one of the most stunning feats of *The Princess of 72nd Street* is that our narrator is always a reliable one. One might call into question the reliability of a character with the kind of magical thinking that leads to dancing topless in Riverside Park for "all of life, all living things and for the sick to make them better," or who believes the red light of a yacht is shining just for them. Yet, both the Princess and Ellen tell the reader the exquisite and ugly truths of the world exactly as they see it. Sane or insane, this is more honesty—imagistic, emotional, and interpersonal—than is conveyed by so many of literature's narrators.

—

MELISSA BRODER is the author of the novels *Milk Fed, The Pisces,* and *Death Valley;* the essay collection *So Sad Today;* and five poetry collections, including *Superdoom.* She has written for *The New York Times, Elle,* and *New York* magazine's *The Cut.* She lives in Los Angeles.

THE PRINCESS OF 72ND STREET

I am glad I have the radiance. This time I am wiser. No one will know. Perhaps it is a virus—a virus causing my being to expand and glow instead of causing nausea and weakness. It is not what they think it is. Usually they treat this lovely feeling with drugs. Weren't they surprised when the lithium salts didn't work. All of them so sure they could call it manic-depression and level it with those salts. I fooled them. Finally it was cured in the usual way. In fact any feeling can be cured if you want to get rid of it by shooting up large amounts of Thorazine, Stelazine, and more recent derivatives into the buttocks or ass or bottom or *gluteus maximus.*

What a fool I was to go there all by myself of my own free will last time and live in the green painted room until they made certain that the radiance was gone. When I have this condition it is hard for me to follow directions, difficult to keep to schedules, to play follow the leader. When they cure it with the drugs that make my limbs heavy and my mind stupified, I cannot laugh suddenly or cry or even dance. It is like something is binding me. But I can follow orders very well. I can do whatever I am told. Then they say, she is over the acute stage. I am praised and the dosage is lowered. Finally I am released. I come out into the world with correct patterns of speech, and for a while I see a psychiatrist and take my maintenance dosage and look for a job in the newspaper. It is a pretense. The realization of who I am comes back to me. Not the radiance. You see, the two don't always go together. I am the Princess of 72nd Street. This is a fact. Something I know deep inside but only mentioned during my first and second radiance. They want me to believe that a radiance follows some terrible rejection or loss of self-esteem and is some kind of defensive device creating chemical changes and loss of boundaries. They are wrong. I have gotten the radiance when I have been depressed about something and also when things were going along in their normal way. The truth that they refuse to admit to is that there is no pattern. None.

For example, I was visiting some friends in the country, somewhere covered with green, somewhere people are proud to live because it is covered with green grass instead of ordinary pavement. This is something I don't understand—arrogance about life near trees and birds and green grass. I've tried. All that green was so dull, so stifling. I had the feeling that the green was sucking up all the air and then spitting out something sickly sweet. But they felt that I should be happy to get away from the city which they think is noisy and smells bad. And so I made the appropriate remarks. Somewhere there must be a book full of them. I learned those things a long time ago. In the evening, to my horror because I hate eating outside, my friend's husband decided that a barbecue was what I would like. A large lump of meat was placed on some tin contraption, and he kept turning it over with an air of self-importance if I remember correctly. I sat around getting nauseated. I like little pieces of meat eaten quickly inside. My friend Melita was doing things to radishes and lettuce, running inside and outside and upstairs and downstairs, as though it were an occasion. She was wearing a pair of the earrings that she makes in the cellar. Melita has a tiny face and a large tall body. The earrings were long almost shoulder length silver loops with three purple plastic triangles just brushing her shoulders. I've never cared for my friend Melita but we think we like each other. It's a friendship that has been going on since she chose to be my friend at an art school where we were studying to be great painters.

In those days Melita painted plums—three plums on a horizontal canvas, or one plum all alone on a square canvas, or plums scattered about, or plums cut open, and occasionally plums on a white plate. When plums were out of season Melita got upset and sat in a corner of the studio. She said she didn't understand life or her own feelings or the feelings in the paintings around her. She over ate during these times, and pimples came out on her back and face. Once I suggested to her that she paint the soul of a plum. She was very suspicious and thought I was being condescending, which I was, but I was also trying to help her pimples. Melita thought about it for a long time and began stretching enormous canvases on which she painted what looked like a sky with a gigantic purple moon. She painted so many of these that she became exhausted and got mononucleosis. Everyone got mononucleosis in those days, but it was probably other things. I think we learned how to induce and produce mononucleosis at will. It was an ultimate solution. Everyone understood, having had it, and everyone was kind and expected nothing. You could have mononucleosis as long as you wanted to. It was better than the way they used to get tuberculosis in the old days. No one died and yet it was long and languorous.

Melita looked beautiful only when she had mononucleosis. She became slim with her whole body going together without lumps of fat or pimples, and her eyes became large and luminous. That is when Peter noticed her—this very same Peter who was turning the lump of meat over and over and now tended to ignore Melita except when they had company. At that time Peter used to go into the woods to shoot rabbits and ducks which he quicky painted in large sure strokes so he was finished in time to eat them. He was known as the genius, the Manet, of our entire group. No one else could paint so quickly with each stroke being the right choice like a miracle. One day for no reason Peter couldn't paint anymore. He couldn't remember how he had been doing it. He stopped hoping for it to come back and studied art history. Even now he teaches courses in art history. His specialty is Vermeer. I don't know why. Vermeer has nothing to do with ducks or rabbits or even plums. No one ever mentions Peter's old paintings. Melita is self-conscious about painting in front of Peter so she makes peculiar jewelry and secretly paints plums when they are in season. I suspect that Peter knows about it, but he never talked about it, at least not then. Peter couldn't stand the sight of a plum. Melita explained to me that she must be very careful because he can smell a plum miles away and breaks out in hives.

They enjoy swimming in their pool. This is something else that I never understood. I think, in fact, that it is crazy, this moving back and forth in water. Even though we are related to the fish in the embryonic stage, I still think it is unnecessary. I watched them the morning after the barbecue. In the middle of the night Peter had come into my bed. I told him that I love Melita too much to do such a thing. It was easier that way. Peter sulked but finally said that he understood. He understands nothing—nothing of my peculiar morality, nothing of my status as Princess of 72nd Street, and nothing of the irrelevant fact that he repels me. The next morning he was holding Melita's wet body near the edge of the pool. I don't swim, just sit dangling my toes in the water. I was watching them swimming back and forth like crazy people with their lips getting blue, both of them thinking there was something good in this. I tried to think of what it could be: gills, legfins, primeval slime, uric acid. Was there some sense of accomplishment they felt? Was it a purely physical sensation, or simply a habit? It certainly made them look ugly and goose-pimpled and blue-lipped and out of breath and wrinkled and pathetic.

Sitting there and watching them I unexpectedly got the radiance. My body felt light as a flower, my breathing itself gave me great pleasure, and my hair seemed to fly up and outward like wispy silk. I smiled and then laughed. Peter and Melita looked up and laughed also. Such musical sounds. Little bells. I began to run around and around on the hot dry grass and to look straight up into the sun. The sun understands me. The sun is a wine fire with strange threads of blue. It roars its comprehension of everything I am. I knew that. Peter and Melita became two exotic wet water flowers simple and spreading out white petals. I embraced both of them.

Neither of them liked this. They know me as someone who is not demonstrative. Peter muttered something about how the country air was doing me good and Melita asked if I was hungry. People like to pretend that radiance is something else when they see it. I hardly heard them. I was leaping and singing and reciting poetry—the poetry of sun and fishfins and balloons. I jumped into the pool and lay there for a long time, smiling at the sun and letting the water fill my ears like it rushes into a seashell. I felt an obstruction and took off my bathing suit, letting it fall to the bottom. I am the water.

I was aware of Peter and Melita who were whispering to each other. Melita has always been angry because my body has no flabby parts and looks as young as it did when we were at art school despite the aging of the internal organs. She took Peter into the house. I noticed these things from a distance as though they were part of a dream. Melita, a shape moving about, came near the pool with a purple towel in her hands. Everything Melita has is purple: her dresses, towels, sheets, mascara, jewelry, shoes, bathing suit. I came right out and into the purple towel and said that I wanted to dance on the lovely wet grass. The grass in reality, in one reality, is ugly and dry, burnt out, and hurts the naked feet. My feet were padded with velvet like the hooves put on horses, so the grass felt soft and wet. I danced away from the towel and Melita like a purple whale was running after me. I thought it was a game and kept on laughing. Melita looked so large and beautiful with her towel.

I must always live here where the sun blooms and the water is purple and the streets are soft and the sun blows love upon both of you and the red meat sizzles on flames so I am not myself as you know me but part of the flame of the sun which is also on the flame-shaped blades of grass, I said. They thought I had gone mad, I suppose, but I knew what was going on at the other level. Sometimes I do. I just couldn't control my radiance which was in my feet and breasts and head and thoughts. I knew that Peter was pacing back and forth looking distraught. The day before Melita had told me about his impotence.

They were whispering about sunstroke. I knew that they would catch me like a butterfly and that I would be imprisoned, but I didn't mind—not even when they did it, scooping me up like a bird when it isn't looking.

Melita made me lie on the bed and gave me aspirins and put a cold towel on my head. Melita doesn't like to take care of people. Peter called the doctor who didn't want to come because it was Sunday. He was probably putting hooks into fish or swimming like a fish or planning a barbecue. He came. They must have told him something alarming or shocking to make him come on a Sunday. He gave me an injection of something to make me stop bothering everyone with my happiness and then he asked me if some problem was upsetting me. I thought this was a funny question and just laughed. I tried to tickle him between the legs and then the drug put me to sleep.

That was one of my early attacks of radiance. The man I had come to the country to get away from and who detested laughing and was appalled by radiance came to take me away. Mistakenly Melita and Peter had summoned him. We drove straight out of the country right up to Bellevue.

I thought Bellevue was beautiful covered with green grass and full of lovely people. I tried to dance with the people on the grass. I told them how happy I was to be there with them and how lucky we were to have the sun shining so warmly on our fingertips. Some laughed or walked away or looked at me. An old man kept blowing up paper bags and then smashing them. I joined him and we both giggled. In a few days they took it from me. It was like a sudden shock with the people looking sick and crying or screaming and the walls turning a dirty green color. The sun was gone and I wanted to get out. It wasn't right. In my opinion radiance is my own and my business and too precious to part with in this world.

—

To live by a morality such as mine would be insane, at least in our times. People would throw stones at me, laugh, put me in solitary confinement, or send me to a behavioral psychologist to be changed. I never mention it. I have never given voice to my deep inner beliefs. Who has? Nor do I live by them—not exactly, not nearly. Before the radiance overwhelms me, now once and for all, I want to tell how I really think about things. I mean things relating to men and women. It takes some courage, understand, particularly since the flittering things are beginning to tickle the inside of my head. First of all if a man is with a woman—even walking down the street or sitting in a restaurant—he should not be permitted to look at the faces or bodies of other women. I would have his eyes put out. Men should be blind. This is something I have worked over in my mind after taking careful note of the way they use their eyes. They cannot focus, have in fact darting eyes, spinning thorny eyes. If a married man looks at a woman younger than his wife or prettier or even of the same prettiness, then he shall forever dwell in darkness. It makes perfect sense. Marriage is sacred although no one dares to admit it. If a man who is married should lie with another woman, then I would have him castrated. What lies behind this morality is not cruelty—quite the contrary. The highest ideals of love, kindness, and felicity to one's mate lie therein.

When a man walking down 72nd Street with a woman let his darting eyes stick to any part of me I used to shout, look at the woman you are with you greedy, eye-darting fool. Now I am silent, not wanting to cause more pain or heartache to the woman since she may not have noticed. Let me say I hate this quality in men and most men have it except those who are nearly blind, totally blind, or without side vision. Many times have I taken great pains with my appearance and dress when with some particular man, only to have him suddenly screech some vulgar sound, hiss, whistle, or moan when he sees a woman who looks the reverse of myself. Or ignoring my beauty, which is being appreciated by men with other women, he will leer at a poster, at a girl in torn jeans, at anything and everything. This has hurt my feelings in the past. One of my lovers seeing me small and exotic, like a true Princess of 72nd Street West must be, developed a yearning for "tall Nordic goddesses," as he so crudely put it. I have matured and adapted to my society and its men, so I simply lowered my eyes. To comment, I have learned, only fouls the air further.

If you marry a man for money then you don't have to concern yourself. Every man will make both the most beautiful or the most homely woman, according to current standards, feel unattractive most of the time. I don't think they do it purposely or unconsciously. It is in their eyes.

The women who go about barefaced, scrubbed clean with tiny eyes and no lips in the name of what is called the women's movement are saying, like me for what I really am. Well they are fools! No one likes anyone for what they really are. But even if they were to improve their faces as they used to, they would get the same result. Then why not remove the eyes of men so that they might sense the souls of women and focus better.

I am also severe, though not quite as punitive with members of my own sex. They don't have such mobile eyes. Any woman who breaks up a marriage by enticing or bewitching a married man should be exiled. Let those women live together on an island far away from all men. When a woman is introduced to another woman's lover or husband she ought not pay attention to him. She should speak in a dull voice of dull things to his wife. Her eyes must be lowered at all times. Some of our women, unfortunately, are most attracted by those who belong to another, liking to play for power or act out father-fixations. These should be banished or deprived of estrogen and progesterone. In my experience of watching everything, women's eyes and attention do not often stray to other men—at least hardly so in proportion to the sins of the male. Still if everyone were blind, would they not make better choices by sound, be less prejudiced, and pay attention to the person they are at the movies with? What then of painting? Perhaps those truly dedicated to painting might keep their eyes in return for voluntarily giving up sexual activity through slow deletion of the proper hormones. Then who would look at their paintings? Let future, more civilized people who have earned the right to have eyes look upon them. Meanwhile sculpture, music, and literature can flourish with the aid of braille.

As you may have concluded, I am an absolutist about monogamy, about fidelity, about eternal relationships. As for those who like people of their own sex, sexually, I would prefer that they also marry and form perfect unions.

While having this morality, this humanistic, ethical morality, I must endure the agony of seeing it defiled day after day by almost everyone and by everything in print. I am forced, yes forced, to make my way in this terrible world of covetous eyes and greedy fingers. Necessity has made me try to see individual cases, be sympathetic to weaknesses—even to have affairs with men who are in love with every female in the world, with several, or with one living in their head who has never been born. I tolerate conversations in which my lover listens, with his eyes on someone else's naked back or buttocks while I am expressing my deepest ideas. And despite my position and my morality, I have discovered myself to be making love with someone who is whispering things about a woman he saw on a subway poster, a child whose panties he pulled down when he was ten, or about an imaginary girls' gymnasium with pubescent girls chinning, lifting weights, and playing volleyball in strange costumes. Men have a need to communicate these visions during intercourse. The alternative is total isolation. Perhaps total isolation is best. It is no comfort to me that other eyes are invading my body or putting me into erotic fantasies when I am not present. Watch those married men who take their children to the zoo on Sunday. Watch their eyes and you will see the horror of it. Evidently they believe themselves starved of a million pulchritudinous behinds and other artifacts of freedom.

—

The radiance is coming slowly this time only making me feel giddy and lighthearted for a second and then fading.

If I, in my imperfect humanity, should happen to be attracted to someone else's husband, I never even look at him though he may think I am rude. I never listen to what he says. I wear clothing that flattens out my breasts when he is near. Yes, I carry many of my principles into practice. Of course I have slept with some married men in my time. Who hasn't? Often they were lame or having a nervous breakdown or extraordinarily persuasive. It is wrong, absolutely wrong, even though married men are usually superior lovers, humbly attentive, and fall in love with a maniacal intensity bordering on insanity, particularly if it is their first transgression. Sometimes the fact of marriage is well hidden or omitted. Even someone like me doesn't suspect until after the fact. Married men should be required by law to wear a special cap which cannot be removed without removing the scalp and a tattoo across the groin saying MARRIED. Then you could stop in time if you have any sense of right and wrong.

You can see how difficult life is for me in an amoral society. But remember—no one knows how I feel. It is stated here for the first and the last time. I also adhere to the principle of an eye for an eye. Too much time is wasted turning the other cheek so it too can be smacked. Everyone should reread the ten commandments as given to Moses, particularly the one about not coveting thy neighbor's wife. I detest divorce and all those who have any part in it. Were I your president I would make divorce illegal except for some very peculiar and weird circumstances such as being driven insane or suicide.

—

The radiance drifts blue circles around my head. If I wanted to I could float up and through them. I am weightless. My brain is cool like rippling waves. Conflict does not exist. For a moment I cannot see—the lights are large orange flowers.

The burdens and duties of being Princess of West 72nd Street are awesome. Yet to the mind of the average person my duties are absurd or nonexistent. Responsibility is one's own affair isn't it? I take my responsibilities very seriously. As to the matter of appearance, for example, I am very exacting. No one could fail to recognize me. Day or evening I wear a floor-length skirt patterned with flowers, cascades of color, or abstract designs. Nothing I wear looks part of any current fashion, nothing is in what is called "good taste," or expensive, or *à la mode.* On the Eastside, merely a short walk across Central Park, I would look like a foreigner. No Wall Street executive, officer of loans, or Madison Avenue ad man would feel any rapport. I am very careful about such misidentifications. With my skirt I wear a tank top leotard, formfitting and simple. Hanging from my neck is a huge medallion. What the medallion represents is inconsequential. Sometimes it is a cross, a star of David, an Egyptian ankh, an astrological symbol, male-female insignia, an ancient coin, crushed metal found in the garbage, an elephant, a racehorse, an owl. As long as it is heavy and large and hanging on a chain it can be mistaken, as I wish it to be, for the neck pendants worn by ordinary Westsiders. One of the difficult tasks of dressing to fulfill my title is firstly to blend with my kingdom—this means to be almost inconspicuous yet easily recognized as a resident. On the other hand it is necessary that I stand out clearly. This is easy since my clothes have the rich patina of a constant costume rather than the fresh look of a new purchase. I never look as though I am wearing a new acquisition. Age has given everything I own a subtle glow. My hair is long and black and my features are made up, not according to the latest dictates of fashion, but according to my singular unchanging concept. Thick black lines, almond-shaped, define my glittering eyes, and dark eye shadow blended with specks of gold colors my lids. My lips, although carefully outlined, are never dark red. They are pale pink blended with white. It would be unthinkable for my ears to be naked. Never. A huge mysterious earring always hangs from each pierced lobe.

I know the feel, the flow, the mood of my little domain better than anyone else. To be casually glamorous and to have a face that the Italians think is Italian, Jews think is Jewish, the Spanish think is from Madrid, and Orientals think is Chinese, and so forth, is what makes it possible for me to float along meeting with no assaults or hostility. It is obvious to everyone that I belong. The people who would assault or mug or whatever, stop when I pass. I walk regally and look somehow beyond being a victim. They know a victim when they see one. As I approach such a group I take on some of their own characteristics chameleon-like and waft through. Anger and hostility dissipate and they separate leaving a space for me to pass. It would not occur to any man to hit me over the head. When in danger I have a glazed look that I place over my eyes; my pupils dilate and I am easily taken for a drug addict.

My eyes can pierce right through to the heart of a problem and reduce the offenders or would-be offender to bewildered passivity. The fist unclenches and the gun drops to the floor. Arrogance is very dangerous in my kingdom. But I project a special dignity which no one would care to defile or tamper with. You have seen the face of the Virgin Mary Mother of Christ on the Sistine ceiling. I never wear a brassiere. It is not a political statement or a protest against the bonds of femininity—it is suited to my area. Anyone who wears a brassiere on West 72nd Street is suspect. The Eastsiders try to effect such Westside understatement. They cannot achieve it and ought not go walking about without their bras. Even I, when traveling to the Eastside will wear one. It is like doing what the Romans do in Rome or avoiding a commotion. A credit to my people, I have been taken for a hooker, Sabra, American Indian, actress, ballerina, witch, holy saint, mother, girl, mystic, ethereal spirit, bitch, earth goddess, and more. All these compliments prove my perfect eligibility for rule in this particular part of the universe.

Everyone knows me and yet I am never overly familiar. I mean with the bartenders, hairdressers, camera store owners, small grocers, embalmers, laundromat operators, T.V. repairmen, and other ordinary citizens.

One thing I should make very clear is that I have nothing to do with Central Park, not even the bicycle or jogging paths, not even the 72nd Street entrance. I dislike its easy accessibility to the East. I am more inclined to include Riverside Park—the 72nd Street area, even extending to the yachts bobbing along in filthy water. Sometimes my realm extends further North as in that case, or further South as regards the Lincoln Center Fountain Ledge which I own. Technically though, my kingdom is straight up and down 72nd Street.

If a new establishment opens up on my street I observe it carefully before deciding whether or not it will become embedded. It must have the correct flavor. Eastsiders occasionally infiltrate from across the park and open up bars and restaurants. These are usually doomed to failure. Such was The Buffalo Bar. It was affected from the start, poorly run—a hybrid, a disaster. It belonged on the Eastside and never attracted people from 72nd Street and the immediate, surrounding areas. Sometime ago it was sold and is now a gay bar. Like The Continental Baths once were, it is in business for money. I object to money as a *raison d'être* or end in itself.

—

For the past five minutes I have been a water lily. Sometimes I become a flower or a moth.

—

Tweed's Bar was an exception. It definitely belonged here, wove itself into the neighborhood and attracted the fine edge people—those film makers who talk film but never make one, some film makers who actually do, residents who do nothing or once did something, actors and actresses waiting on line, overly casual psychologists, and a few self-made mystics. Altogether too many lawyers invaded, I believe. It closed because of a murder while I was locked up for having my last radiance, Number 6. Now it is called The Big Apple Café and is ambivalent as to clientele. It is dangerous to be away. Places like Tweed's disappear and others such as Kentucky Fried Chicken or the sordid Blimpie Base appear. Needless to say, a McDonald's or a Kentucky Fried Chicken concession has no business on this street. A little further away, on Columbus between 72nd and 71st or thereabouts is Bagel Nosh, another new, demented chain restaurant which had its origins in the East and has no business taking up space. Walter B. Cooke and The Blarney Castle can remain as far as I'm concerned.

A bookstore finally opened a few years ago while I was away. There was a desperate need among my people. I have promoted it, inhabited it, helped it take root just by my presence and patronage within. That is my mysterious power. At first it looked pristine, anxious, lacked the comfortable veneer of anyplace destined to survive here. At my silent insistence it was darkened, scratched, made to look warm and womblike, and eventually dedicated itself to crazy mystics and Sufi. I know my people. They will not even notice a clean cold-looking store or one that wants their money. Not even if they are hungry for books. It needs antiquing, old rugs, wicker chairs, a few relics, a coffee urn, an amber feeling. Just as the real residents of my empire have a worn Mesopotamian flavor so must the stores. This is not a country for Nordic blondes of impeccable taste and pearly white skin. Bergdorf Goodman wouldn't last a minute. Admittedly they will be stared at and propositioned. But they will never be taken in. The very essence of the streets is in opposition. I have known them to migrate from the Eastside and then to move back quite rapidly. They never understood the rules—couldn't find the rhythm. This is true of Eastside men who come to our O'Toole's Saloon as though it were The Purple Plum or other Eastside singles' bar. Inevitably they are ostracized. The hardcore Westside woman does not respond to a bed-or-nothing approach, although here we are more passionate than elsewhere. We don't like to be bullied by slick strangers in Gucci jeans. We don't like a glib line, a swagger, an ostentatious stance at the bar, an obvious perusal. The rhythm is wrong. If the rhythm is wrong the true Resident can feel it immediately. We on West 72nd Street have our own particular pace and sense of aptness.

I have to know all these things—moods, changes, innuendos. I am the first to freeze out an enthusiastic Eastsider who has heard things about the Westside and who comes to scoop them up. The disguise is usually wrong. We like our sooty streets with outdoor tables put right down among the garbage bags. Go back to the Hamptons. Or worse yet, to the cocktail lounges of Queens and Manhasset. Oh, sometimes, it becomes a burden and a worry. If I should move away it would fall apart. Strangers would infiltrate. The celebrities would no longer be able to stroll about unseen, coming out of the Dakota in jeans and sitting in the Oedipus luncheonette like anyone else.

I hold together this subtle pattern of existence with my energy and essence. It is imperative that I stay here despite the cost to my nerves, despite the work involved.

Our gay people can hold hands as they walk and most of them do not feel segregated, nor do our insane or unemployed or successful or unsuccessful. This is a place where the last thing you ask someone is what they do. Anyone who asks someone how they get their money is definitely on the wrong street. Intelligence and achievements are carefully hidden. There is no air of bravado. No one bothers the stars of the soaps as they eat prefrozen hamburgers in our major luncheonette, the Oedipus, on the corner of 72nd Street and Columbus. As for the ABC staff, playwrights, eyewitness news team, novelists, prima ballerinas, pop culture heroes—they can go back and forth quite anonymously. It depends upon how you want to live. When Melita looks at the street it is with disgust. She smells the garbage that is often left to rot and cannot understand how or why I remain. No use explaining it to her. If we need a tree we grow a small palm or elm in our apartments. Tomatoes and radishes grow in boxes placed on dirty windowsills. A tan can be gotten free in Riverside Park, and there are always places open for late night wanderers. This is our own utopia or fantasyland. We would be lost in the Everglades.

Don't ever listen to rumors about what used to be called "Needle Park" but is really a place where the old and weary rest their feet. As for murders, some of my best friends were murdered and raped on the elegant Eastside.

—

Soft hissing waves run over my toes. The floor is a beach and I am rolling on the sand and splashing in the water with a white heron. It turns gray and blue. No one can stop this. No one will take away my radiance even when it floods over me completely.

—

When Melita was painting plums and only plums, and Peter was shooting and painting rabbits and ducks, I was painting tangerines, brown teapots, rolls, and books. These objects were unstill, scattered about falling and flying—not purposely but because of something inside me. I was so intense about the whole thing, trying to get at something, painting in nervous threadlike strokes. My vision was peculiar in the way El Greco's vision is said to have been. Perhaps it was a small defect in my brain or on the retina or in the relationship between all those things. I was unable to see the true sizes of things. Sometimes the roll was enormous with huge greenish black seeds and the teapot was tiny and the colors in the white tablecloth seemed to dance out so that there was every color except white. I was never the type who could paint a tablecloth white with a gray shadow or use two or three colors for a tangerine. That was my major problem. Melita had an opposite defect. She stuck to one thing and to one or two colors. I envied Melita. Her view of the universe was simple. What to do if in fact the white tablecloth had as many colors as the tangerine and on top of that the teapot was no color at all—just a mass of reflections? It all tended to drive me crazy.

It was a conservative school and no one was painting abstractly. Philadelphia is slower to catch up with things. The instructors never mentioned abstract expressionism. I suppose they were afraid we would all start disregarding objects and then they wouldn't know what to do. It is only now that the obsolete boring hard edge is in vogue in Philadelphia. It took a long time for the miniskirt to get there.

—

I have just informed the shopkeepers, ad-libbed and gone into unnecessarily elaborate explanations about a short vacation I am taking, a cruise around the world, a sort of holiday. I mentioned nothing about my radiance to them. I feel that some sort of explanation is due people who depend upon my daily excursions and appearances. Ordinarily I would keep on with my duties but that leads to trouble. I don't have much self-control and even now when I have it under control, so to speak, and am also going to experience it, I must be certain not to cause myself to be seen until I have passed the crest. I feel no less dignified but judging from past reactions and recalling incidents or learning about them later, it seems that my behavior does undergo certain changes. I hate to admit this and it does disturb me—now before I am completely within it—but my morality undergoes certain changes. Things are not as clear. I even forget the ten commandments as were given to Moses. These lapses may cause certain people to conclude that I am not fit to be sovereign ruler of West 72nd Street. I learned from Melita, for instance, that I had pulled Peter's penis. Imagine that, and Peter being married for so long. Not that it would do any good, she had added, trying to make light of something serious in its implications.

Don't assume that my entire morality dissolves with my radiance. That is unthinkable. I know right from wrong. There is no question about that. I simply feel lighthearted and everything has an aura of bubbles. Life itself seems rather comical and sweet—not absurdly or grotesquely funny—but a lighthearted event. Obstructions such as marriages and people's individual moods no longer pose all sorts of questions, problems, and barriers. My head doesn't hurt. Never confuse this with a mystical or cosmic experience like something reported by Indian Masters or those meditating all day or starving themselves. I have never meditated or gone in for mysticism. I have always believed in facing cold reality and have never sought eternal bliss through the teachings of Zen Masters or through mind-expanding drugs. I don't need LSD for things to look pretty.

That this particular thing descends upon me is purely accidental. If it is a gift I accept it gladly. I am not going into a mental hospital this time to have them take it away with Thorazine. But it is not going to be easy to have the radiance and watch my behavior at the same time.

After my last seizure or state of grace, I wrote down a plan which I can now refer to. It contains a list of places where I must not go and people I must not see and sentences that I must practice since ordinary language seems to evaporate. I have to struggle with proper speech at this time. Also there is a clothing check before I go out and a general rule of silence. It is important not to blab too much and clothing tends to annoy me. I forget parts or cannot, as much as I try, seem to think of any reason for wearing coverings. I have no suicidal or homicidal feelings at this time—I only have those when I am so-called sane.

In order to keep the attack, the radiance, the gift, the psychosis if you insist, under control I must focus upon one thing, concentrate all my attention on a single task. This is very difficult if anyone could appreciate the difficulty. Just now, for example, my toes called attention to themselves, seemed to be wrapped in dark red velvet shoes inside and out. My toes wanted to get up and dance, but I have it under control, for the moment at least, and instead of dancing in the hallway, inside the elevator, or on the marble streets, I crossed my legs beneath me—quite harshly in fact. I must concentrate because even between sentences or words my fingers begin to take on the white soft texture of orchid petals. They want to stroke things. So I must reason with them, tell them they are in fact flesh and bone and should stay on the typewriter keys. It is too bad isn't it that society is so intolerant of changes in personality—so much so that I must stay here working, telling instead of fully experiencing the radiance. It shows. Never think it is something that can be hidden. The police are what concern me and incarceration and of course my tainted reputation as royalty.

Here now my ordinary chair—straight-backed black wood with a stapled-on blue felt seatcover—turns into a throne. Not a stable throne but one that swings from the ceiling by two heavy chains. Carved cupids play about its arms and legs, and woven gold pillows make it soft and fit for my body which is now marble white; it no longer has the usual pigmentation with a dark sunspot here and there, a tiny crease, a stretched vein, a flaw, an uneven fleshtone. There are no pores or anything. I am white consistently as I swing upon my throne laughing and stroking the cupids with my sensitive petaled fingers. How strange that people cut and file nails and that nails grow at all. Most peculiar are fingers and toes. The press insists that the hand has beauty, even Michelangelo with the thumb in opposition, as though that were a big deal because the monkeys don't have it. Cats wouldn't be seen with an opposing thumb. Everything is artistically subtle and hidden with soft fur. I am not supposed to think this way. Only the typewriter can help me now. I am clever, and even before this when I was ordinarily, quietly Princess, I constructed a system of ropes or clothes lines. Now they save me, leading from the typewriter to the Frigidaire, or from the typewriter to the bathroom. I hold on to these ropes very tightly with those fingers you are all so proud of and grope along. If not I would never return to the typewriter. I hate it.

The danger is dispersion and activities seen as aberrant by the authorities. I have my money laid out in piles: pennies, nickels, dimes, quarters, dollars, and so on. A big sign says MONEY IS THE MEANS OF BARTER. I forget things like that.

This, by the way, is my seventh radiance and as you know seven is a magic number. During my fourth or fifth radiance, I floated happily, laughingly into one of my grocery stores. Everyone was smiling, although they tried not to show it, because their Princess had entered. It's not polite to stare at royalty. Oh, but they were humble and honored, and I could see that they were watching secretly and even following me about to get a better look. It isn't often that dressed in such finery I will enter the Ruxton whose name has been changed to Parkwest Delicatessen. It is a small, very expensive market or a cross between a grocery store, supermarket, and delicatessen. I was wearing something translucent, long and white, flaming white with green satin-covered dancing shoes. I was in the mood to be generous to those I rule, so I decided to gather whatever was white, which included white bread, toilet paper, paper plates, candles, eggs. I remember weeping because the fruits were not white, then looking again and realizing that if seen in opposition—that is—opposite to the way I used to paint white tablecloths, these fruits were by nature of their color pure white especially when spinning.

I waved my hand which was a flower of some kind without an opposing thumb, and the apples became white with sap or juice flowing forth, and the limes were also white and the grapefruits, so huge and round, became silver just like parting the Red Sea. Next I gathered everything in my skirts, thanked the people who surrounded me with pushcarts, and proceeded to distribute my treasures to my subjects outside. Not to the poor rather than to the rich—that distinction is actually a prejudice and true only in a narrow economic sense like the opposing thumb. They were all thankful. But people came from the store and screamed at me. I thought they meant that I should take more things, not just in my beautiful skirt, but in one of their magic carts. So I returned graciously and sweetly smiling, only to be arrested. Not that I realized it.

I was arrested and it soon became apparent to my representatives of the law that I did not understand what it was all about except for brief seconds. There are always those. They were not mean. They were in fact policemen of my own kingdom and they knew me and had guessed at my royal nature. The policemen are not the way you think policemen are if you are susceptible to propaganda. I am not and wish you weren't. Marriage is good, for example, and the food in the supermarket is not so full of awful chemicals that you must shudder in disgust and buy birdseed and roots in special stores in order to live. You don't even have to jog. From me you will hear the truth rather than propaganda. It is my royal sense of honor.

I cannot lie—not even when it comes to the question of tall people. I am sorry to hurt the feelings of tall people in my kingdom and without. Some of my best friends and lovers are tall. But if you study the matter carefully you will notice that small people, both men and women, are prettier, in better proportion, look younger, and are sweeter and more generous than tall ones. It is better to be short than tall. If you use the eyes that no one entitled you to have and which I may take away in time, you can study the grace and beauty of small limbs. Some of the greatest choreographers have lost their sense of proportion, unfortunately. But not the jockeys on thoroughbred horses. This time, Radiance 7, I will place diamond necklaces around the tiny necks of all the midgets in my kingdom. In my kingdom most of the residents are short. I wonder who started the rumor of tall being better or handsomer or prettier with so much leg and neck and long arms? Probably the economists who are responsible for the sale of badly written books and the promotion of rotten pianists and violinists instead of the true artists who are collecting unemployment on West 90th Street.

It is wrong to be prejudiced, but in my radiance it seems perfectly right that the tall should be put into exile for some years or tossed into the park leading to the Eastside. Most of them live there anyhow—the tall executives, bank presidents, conservative lawyers, and other mechanical giants. Tall people, being greedy, make most of the money. The fact that I am short has nothing to do with it. I am perfectly capable of objectivity in scientific matters. This peculiar habit of taste has puzzled me for long years. Cleopatra, Helen of Troy, and Aphrodite, to name a few, were all five feet and two inches. Apologies to my tall acquaintances and friends who look so much older than they are, walk with ungainly strides, seem about to topple over, and use up so much cloth to cover themselves. What a waste. I am trying to stick to a point, and now I have lost the point which is a symptom of my state of grace, as I like to call it.

The point I have retraced is that I can be easily arrested during radiance because according to law and order I am out of order. From that to Bellevue or Roosevelt Hospital or even St. Vincent's, if I wander too far, is a short interval. Excuse my lack of cohesion. Unfortunately my urge to gather things increases and is almost a warning of what is to come. It doesn't always take place at once, in an instant, I mean like when I was dangling my feet in the pool while visiting Peter and Melita. Sometimes there is a warning, an aura, a slow building.

Several days ago, after a series of what I would call normal despondencies, my spirits rose. I walked down 72nd Street noting that all was particularly well with the exception of the Argentinian pianist who sells records. He keeps his eye on me and I keep my eye on him and once I became too friendly. A certain distance suits my position better. Perhaps I hurt him. What I mean is a year ago after an intimate discussion about the arts and a display from him of his piano virtuosity and old clippings, all in back of the store, I continued to walk by with only a nod, hello, or less. No more discussions or auditions. This is how I am. Not that I have any lack of concern. As I was saying, and then was interrupted by an almost uncontrollable urge to run into Riverside Park and swing up in the trees, I noticed that he had lost weight, was indeed emaciated, and had a lusterless look. It depressed me despite my good spirits. I have great plans for his future but problems working them out. I should like to place a green velvet cape about his shoulders and send him for a physical examination. But nothing was amiss. I felt that it was necessary to adorn myself, kept stopping everywhere buying things and being very talkative which are definite warnings.

I stopped in a cheap store that buys, sells, and fixes radios almost at the corner of Broadway. It was glistening with inexpensive junk jewelry, fairly bursting with ornaments. I bought the largest and cheapest rings—bright fake stones set in tin—one for every finger. The sun broke the glass into rainbows. It has nothing to do with saving money. My taste changes. I should have realized radiance had come. I found myself wearing a large acid green straw hat from the Japan Art Center, a black necklace with blue, orange, and white stones, an arm band of cheap alloy, not to mention five key chains containing dice, peace symbols, and naked people with flags. I bought other things—mainly gaudy dresses with sequins that I ordinarily wouldn't like, Wonder Woman comic books, and records of the Criminals, Bootstrap Five, Ass-stompers, Orange Musk, Hospital Demons, Nude Playbirds, Foul Cheese, Clocktappers, and other new punk rock groups. I knew what I was doing. Although I listen almost exclusively to classical music, I thought it was time to catch up on the contemporary scene so I might know what the younger people of my kingdom were "into."*

August is so beautiful on West 72nd Street and I just savored, almost swallowed and drank it. In fact I chatted with the people who frequent Orange Julius at the corner of 72nd Street and Broadway. I was so happy to be there. It had the feeling suited to my mood. I spoke about jewelry to a woman who looked like a man or a man dressed as a woman or transformed into the other and invited her to come for dinner. Such a willingness to converse always impresses me nor do I mind if someone decides to become one of the other sexes medically. I was spontaneous and warm the way people should be. In all ways I was me. It seems so. Walking back up to Columbus a darling little old man stopped to chat with me. He was selling watermelons or delivering them in a big truck. Ordinarily I wouldn't have stopped. The fact that I did and gave him my phone number is peculiar in a way. But it was beginning and Tony and the watermelons looked right together. It was like giving my phone number to all short old men and watermelons. Something like that, full of truth

* Into—in common use since 1964 meaning involved in, but implying short sudden interest and infidelity. I do not accept this word.

and eternity. He was delighted calling after me as I went up the street bedecked in all my cheap jewels. The sun was so hot on my tin rings. The sidewalks were marble, had no delineations of concrete slabs.

I knew it was on its way and I laughed all the way up in the elevator. Then I pressed my lips together and sat very still and gathered up my notes and plans and resolutions and knew that this, my seventh radiance, would be unlike the other six. I would have it while not acting it out, and keep writing if it killed the petals of my fingers. I vowed not to go out naked or try to cut down trees or take gifts from strangers unless I handed out money. Right now if you asked me what money means I couldn't tell you, except that if I hand it out when I pick up gifts from the Greek luncheonette or Parkwest Delicatessen, I will not be arrested. The phone is ringing but I must not answer because I might do whatever I am asked, or invite someone strange up. Peter is smart and knows or senses when. I am talking about Melita's Peter.

I slipped up today. This is what it could be called although I am very happy and so was the old watermelon man before he left. The buzzer rang without warning and I rang back hardly able to stand it anymore, not knowing if great honors were to be bestowed upon me. I dispersed into petals and laughter and nothing was focused in my eyes. There he was, so old and small and sweating, carrying three ripe watermelons. There were no notes on old men or watermelons. Tony didn't notice anything funny about me, was just pleased and I made him a crown from tin foil that looked beautiful on his head. We danced and shouted, and I didn't care about my neighbor ringing the bell and complaining. He was just doing his duty. Besides I was touched in the heart with the big bursting beauty of the watermelons and something golden poured over everything so nothing was wrong, right, or debatable. If I am pregnant that would be very nice coming from the watermelon pits, and besides if you want to think correctly, young women marry little old producers, directors, high officials, geniuses, senators, and millionaires, so why is it different because Tony works with watermelons? He was full of perfumed sweat from the melon meat and there were no raids or arrests. Trying so hard to reason which, if you don't know, is artificial for me during this time and quite hard, I did manage to reason back at the typewriter that radiance may be something that should be expelled or given off so that it doesn't last forever or clog up and explode. Some of it had been used up with Tony who was a beautiful little king like King Lear if you will. We used the radiance well, particularly if I am pregnant.

Now I am back in focus as much as I can. It isn't as much as when I began but I can get it back with effort. It was different than when Melita's husband comes, and I don't even know if he is or isn't impotent or why. What did she mean by impotence? Peter gets very happy but it is all alone, all about himself and I am not even in it—I am aware of things like that. However I have never been as aware of things as I am now. When Peter came into my room during the night when I was visiting that was different. He didn't know and probably was making a gesture that married men make all the time. I sent him away as I told you before, and I had no radiance until the next day. But Peter came back which I didn't deliberately omit, just forgot in all the excitement. It was embarrassing because he was upset about his impotence and was blaming Melita and her plums. He got on top of me with nothing done in advance and I said nothing. He wanted assistance and I did but nothing happened and he got depressed and went away. It was against all my principles. Why then was he so offended during the radiance when I was affectionate? Is it that men want to have sex potently but don't like affection particularly from the wrong people? During the next radiance he happened to be in the city on 72nd Street before I was incarcerated—if you will—and it has been like that ever since, Peter knowing that I don't have my morality the same way and that I don't even know that word. I don't even know "impotence" while I am writing, except on an intellectual level, because I am straining my head and breaking this radiance into parts, focusing pretty well, all things considered that I am sometimes a plant or covered with pretty feathers or pristine marble. It wouldn't be in my mind to say no to Peter except now when I have made cards that tell me things like SAY NO TO PETER. It might be wrong to do that.

The radiance may be made for the sake of people like Peter and the old watermelon man and the Argentinian concert pianist, not strictly for myself although it is quite pleasant. What if it is really a social event?

I am now tied to the chair because I have a great urge to give a watermelon to the Argentinian pianist and I have forgotten about clothes and cannot figure out whether or not I am dressed correctly for going downstairs. I thought I was dressed so elegantly when I was arrested in the Ruxton but I was wearing an old lacy white nightgown. It couldn't pass for a dress anywhere and nothing was underneath, but I wasn't naked. And I also had on black boots which I thought were green dancing slippers. This improvement is only because I am forced to write and this makes me sound logical. Were I to stop, I don't know what might happen in the elevator with the watermelons. The Argentinian pianist is married and you know how I feel about the sanctity of marriage.

—

I have discovered that my thoughts can become most clear and ordinary when I am thinking about the past. It is the present which breaks up into pieces like lovely flickering white moths.

Everyone has a personal manifestation which if heightened could lead to something dangerous or at least impending. When I was struggling to become a great painter in art school, an instructor attempted to help. He explained that I had to grasp the essential color or group of colors of objects—one in relation to the other like red, blue, and purple. He meant that in my intense vigilance I was, as they say, losing the tree in the forest. It isn't that I was scientific, it was just that I felt the need to tell the truth about everything. If a pot had nine hundred colors I wasn't about to leave one out. He tried harder, showing me reproductions of Cézanne who saw many colors in each thing and yet managed extreme contrasts and a very white tablecloth. Cézanne is not the type of person to paint a tablecloth white with a shadow made of mixed black and white as the cloth goes over the corner. That was my trouble—an inability to accept lies or compromises. By the time I finished looking at a leaf and a glass of water they both had equal parts of green and red and every other color. There was no help for it. I refused to make things easy—to paint a leaf cadmium green with some white in it was out of the question. That is not how it is. My paintings were crazily intense with all those threads of color everywhere. And my head often hurt. You could still see the forms of the leaves, the teapot, and the glass. Somehow it had not gone so far as to have become an unrecognizable mass. I think now that I should have been encouraged even further in my own way, rid myself of all outlines, let the objects fuse. Perhaps I would have experienced the ultimate radiance then—something like those mystics who annoy me greatly.

Maybe things would not have turned out as they have if someone had forced me to make a green leaf all green and a tablecloth gray and white. Maybe that is what I really need even now. I was never one to see the point in inactivity, in waiting for things to happen like someone in a religious trance. I had the greatest disdain for Melita, for her unquestioning takeover of the plum. Her plums were quite purple. There is nothing worse or more deceitful than a purple plum. The absolute arrogance of it.

But if dispersion is a problem, I had it then and have it now and will probably always have it. I also have the radiance. As if this were not enough, there is the opposite side. This is my sense of right and wrong and my utter belief in the ten commandments as given to Moses, particularly the one about men not looking at other women. I used to tell my lover George to go sleep with the woman rather than to drool over her. No one seems to understand that the thought is worse than the act. God understood when He said that men should not covet their next door neighbor's girlfriend. Murder is an exception and should only be thought about. Speaking of the Bible,

I have often thought it would be a good life to be sitting and thinking inside the belly of a whale.

—

Last night I went inside the elevator—not with any purpose in mind except to ride up and down and up and down and to greet the passengers, my subjects who live in the building. Usually I am repelled by close proximity to strangers and stand pressed against the corner hoping that the elevator won't make any unnecessary stops. Last night I skipped lightly into that magic box with blue lights gleaming from its roof and walls of flaming orange. I embraced everyone who came inside: sweet people, the mean ones, old, young, the pushers, heroin addicts, cocaine snorters, drunks, married men, wives, all. Up and down, giving and giving my love for what must have been a long time until a man with greasy hair and patchy blotches, who smelled of oranges or wine took me home. He seemed very gentle and wanted me to take some pills which were red and then he appeared to be pulling me around slapping my cheeks and telling me to wake up. It wasn't Thorazine. Thorazine is not red. His eyes were like tiny lights with no meaning. He was a spice-smelling crawling vine trying hard to grow all around me and inside. It tickled.

Today I have marks that are purple and blue, but nothing hurts from the vine because I don't experience any pain physical or mental during a radiance, which someone once said is dangerous. They don't like it when you have no pain. I don't know who that blotched man was. I wasn't put into Bellevue and he didn't take it away. I liked the old watermelon man better. It wasn't Peter either. I really don't know, and I forgot to read my notes before I embarked. I couldn't stop myself from riding up and down. This morning I read a card while laughing that says DON'T LET STRANGE MEN INTO YOUR APARTMENT. I wonder what I really meant. It might get out of hand you know, but I didn't go outside. Somehow I remembered that outside even in my own kingdom there are people who cannot stand to see such happiness as mine. They don't like it when a person loses the opposing thumb and all those timebound organs and becomes a seaweed or laughs at nothing.

Before I became Princess of West 72nd Street from Central Park West to Riverside Park, I lived with George. We did not live in holy matrimony but in what used to be called sin and should be called sin again before holy matrimony disappears due to press coverage and statistics. Because I am blue and purple I will try to tell about George. George was an academic, which is any bearded man who teaches in a university and who has written or is writing now or for all eternity a dissertation. A dissertation has no value that I can see except to get a doctorate in some subject so you can teach.

Before George, my academics were art historians who are very neat and have problems with sex. Then I tried the sciences such as physics, chemistry, and mathematics. These cannot converse. They are not impotent but clumsy and inept and need to bathe more often and consult a periodontist. In general scientists are boring and cannot convey excitement about anything. In addition they are unusually tall and too thin except for certain mathematicians who think of nothing but mathematics and eating. But I did not give up—I tried the philosophers. The philosophers were all stark raving mad, all in analysis which wasn't helping, and had the most peculiar sexual fetishes and fantasies. Some were dangerous and none of them could finish the dissertation which was about something they couldn't understand and so couldn't write about. Philosophers are also very fond of food and get plump and senile at an early age. After philosophers I had decided to discontinue my search for an academic. At this time I met George while drinking beer in Riis Park, a beach mainly frequented by homosexual men who cannot afford the better places, but having a few areas for heterosexuals.

It was mainly a matter of beards and he had the longest and thickest one that I had ever seen. People made fun of it on the streets. George didn't notice me for a long time although I sat at his table—one of those hot tin tables when you walk up from the sand. George is very nearsighted and has poor side vision both of which were to my advantage after he finally turned his head around and saw me. I suppose he thought he was alone. Later, he barely saw the attractive women he would have otherwise coveted unless, of course, they were right up close in front of him. He was in between a few marriages, as academics are if they marry at all. They have a lot of trouble staying married to one person. Being an expert in such matters, I knew that he was an historian of some kind and that he had no sexual problems. He was amiable for quite some time. I didn't know for months that George was someone who could never be disagreed with. If I disagreed he turned into Frankenstein's Monster—foamed at the mouth, ripped rags, broke bones. For three years I agreed with George, except for sudden relapses, and encouraged him in the writing of that insipid dissertation. I can't remember it now, have permanently forgotten the subject except that it contained Christ, the Russian Revolution, and Lenin. George was Irish but was attracted to Russians and to revolutions. I loved George anyhow, mainly because of his long beard.

—

Things were not going well, and one day if my memory is accurate, George, while working on the dissertation gave me the first of a series of orders. It happened casually, before I even realized. The first thing George announced while stroking his beard, barely glancing up from his desk, was that I was not to sing any longer. I loved to sing but never sang well or particularly often and certainly not when George was working on the dissertation or seemed to be. I walked barefoot, even held my breath so that there would be no sound, no disturbance. And if I was there at all I sat where I could not be seen. George liked to know I was there, silent and unseen. Can I sing when you are in the library or teaching a class about the Russian Revolution or the Communist Manifesto? I asked meekly, first forming the sentence in my mind. It annoyed George if a thought was expressed vaguely or without precision and exactitude. George was silent for a long time with his hands across his chest. I am depressed about your singing, he answered. Then

George put on his Persian hat and Persian gloves and red boots and went out into the snow. I sat there not knowing if I was allowed to sing. Perhaps George will sneak back and listen at the door and hear me sing and go into a rage. George did just that so it was understood that I must not be caught singing under any condition. One day George came back from teaching his class about the Communist Manifesto and the Russian Revolution and announced that he would prefer it if I stopped laughing. I immediately laughed thinking that George had a hidden sense of humor. George's face grew red and he drooled. When George got into a rage he drooled and tore rags. The tearing of rags was an accompaniment suggested by his psychiatrist so that he wouldn't break any more bones by thrusting his hand into the wall. I sat and watched George doing this and didn't think I would ever feel like laughing again anyhow.

I was surprised when George informed me some days later that his psychiatrist wanted to see me. It is true that things were not going well. George barely spoke to me, and I neither sang nor laughed and rarely said anything for fear that the formulation wouldn't be just right. In matters of sex things went well between George and me. In fact it was the only thing that did. Occasionally George would leave a note that said I PROMISE THAT THINGS WILL BE BETTER. LOVE GEORGE. The note was accompanied by flowers or by a dress that was several sizes too large. I loved George, particularly his beard, and was always deeply moved by his notes and gifts. Once he even read the Communist Manifesto to me. And he often read parts of his dissertation which made no sense. I had great faith in our relationship, particularly since George was being treated for his problems by a great psychiatrist.

Doctor Clufftrain was the tallest man I had ever seen. No ordinary doorway was high enough for him to pass through without bruising his nose. He therefore carried a hacksaw so that he could reach up and take a few feet of plaster off the openings he encountered. By contrast the doctor's office was very tiny, although all the doors had been designed to suit his size so he didn't have to hack.

He was extraordinary—a dedicated man who saw patients from 6 A.M. until 3 A.M. I was quite impressed even awed until I met him. While George waited outside in a tiny anteroom where Doctor Clufftrain cooked T.V. dinners between patients, I was beckoned inside by the doctor's long pinky. He took a long time adjusting himself in a seat which was surprisingly low. Doctor Clufftrain was afraid of heights I learned. He trembled and held on to the sides of the chair as though he might suddenly fall out. He twisted his body, checked the back of the chair, and bent down to touch the floor.

After this lengthy preparation he took a deep breath, held it for a while, and then slowly let it out in a hiss. I supposed that he was now ready. He stared at me. He stared at me for a long time twitching his face and muttering obscenities to himself. Then very slowly he got up and holding on to the walls he walked cautiously to his desk. All the while he stared over his shoulder at me. He decided to crawl back on all fours and climbed into his chair sweating and shaking. Holding on to the arms of the chair he leaned toward me and gave me a document and a pen. The document said: Anything I say to Doctor Clufftrain may be used as he sees fit, may be recorded and mailed to anyone, and Doctor Clufftrain is in no way responsible for my well-being.

Wanting to get down to business, I signed this quickly and the doctor put it underneath his chair. George and I have decided that you need some tranquilization to calm you down, he said. His hand shook as he handed me a prescription. I know all about your relationship with George—your excessive demands, upheavals, foaming at the mouth, breaking his bones, insecurities. George is very concerned about you. But George has fits and tantrums and has ordered me not to sing or laugh, I said. Nonsense, said the good doctor. I waited while he had a spasm in which all his muscles twitched. He heaved, choked, and then took a deep breath again, finally letting it out. George is under a great strain. Tension you know. Women always add to his problems. He chooses poorly. One of his wives killed herself—hardly a considerate thing to do.

I wonder if you see any need to continue imposing yourself on him. The doctor looked pleased with himself. I said nothing, suddenly realizing that Doctor Clufftrain might be insane and even dangerous. I glanced up and he was holding his head with both hands trying to stop it from moving back and forth. He looked up. As you must know I am a married man and president of the Society to Preserve Roots, he said. Then he was silent, staring at me again. Was he waiting for me to say something? It was 2:20 A.M. I noticed. The clock hung from the ceiling by a small gold chain. I felt tired and confused. I love George, I said, and Doctor Clufftrain made a sound that could have been a laugh or a gasp. His head fell over to the right side and he went into spasms. And you suppose I don't love George, he suddenly shrieked, turning a bluish color. I treat George free of charge. George is my darling, my pet, my alter ego. George makes my world go round and round. Of course, I said. He was fidgeting with his hacksaw. Any questions? he shouted suddenly, throwing his hacksaw across the room. Is George improving? I asked. Stupid stupid, the very fact, the very idea, I see what the problem is all about. You may go. Doctor Clufftrain remained seated as I opened the doors with some difficulty. George came in and helped Doctor Clufftrain out of his chair. Doctor Clufftrain smiled and patted George's shoulder. See that the prescription is filled, he said.

Isn't he marvelous? George asked with some enthusiasm as we began the journey home. I answered in the affirmative as usual. Does he have a disorder of the nerves or muscles? I asked George fearing the worst. But George was in one of his unpredictable good moods. George was unpredictably in a good mood when things could be blamed on someone else. He's just a sensitive man who vibrates to every emotion that anyone expels, George answered cheerfully. If it weren't for Doctor Clufftrain, I would have killed myself long ago. He has made me see that all flaws lie outside myself.

The druggist had never heard of the pills that Doctor Clufftrain prescribed but he managed to locate them within a week in some experimental laboratory for brain chemotherapy. He looked a little worried when handing me the bottle. George insisted that I take one immediately. I took one and fainted a half hour later. The doctors in the emergency room called Doctor Clufftrain because they had no knowledge of the drug and my pulse was very weak. Doctor Clufftrain told them that it was only an initial effect and that the cure was to give me another one. For several weeks I fainted and threw up and then became very slow in my movements. I thought very quickly while speaking unevenly and haltingly. This has been irreversible. Otherwise there were no ill effects.

—

I became Princess of 72nd Street the moment I stepped off the 104 bus. I was still living with George though more and more often he wanted me out of the apartment. He found the very silence he had created irritating, but if I spoke he went into a rage over the halting way I formed my sentences. Doctor Clufftrain had told George that he needed more time alone and had also reminded him that the apartment was his. I never knew at what hour I would be asked to leave, and even with the door closed he no longer let me paint in the small bedroom.

I had been painting many self-portraits, making certain that I put in a black background to delineate the head. Outlining nose and lips with black was against my principles, but I did not know what else to do. George no longer paid any attention to my work. The years with Doctor Clufftrain had changed him or else he had been feigning interest at the outset. I am not certain. But one day George announced that he had discussed the matter with the doctor and that they had decided that my painting in the bedroom was intrusive, aggressive, hostile, and narcissistic.

It was on that day that I took Broadway Bus 104 to West 72nd Street and got off. I don't know why I got off at that particular street. I could have continued all the way downtown and even across to the East Forties. Isn't it these strange actions—unknown, innocent, spontaneous—that tend to shape our lives?

The streets and the people welcomed me. I found a game club and paid to play Ping-Pong and Scrabble with strangers who became my friends. Having begun to feel unattractive on 114th Street, I felt instantly beautiful on 72nd. The waiters in the Greek luncheonette fussed over me, and a gaunt man with long hair tied with elastic talked to me at the counter. He invited me to see his apartment. It was a tiny room in a commercial building with nothing except a radio, a tape recorder, and a dirty mattress in it. I like simplicity, he explained and added that he had enough money for any kind of apartment. This was his choice—no phone, no ornaments, no furniture or even books. Look, nothing at all, he laughed making a cup of tea with a coil that he plugged into a socket and then placed into his cup. Since he only had one cup we drank taking turns. I felt happy in that room with Anatole. Perhaps his name was really Joe or Al, but he had a right to call himself Anatole, I think. He kept laughing at himself and at his little room while gently stroking my hair. He didn't scream at me or tell me not to laugh. I was no longer in the habit of laughing and, although I felt like it, the reflex was gone. That can happen to tears or laughing or anything with the proper drugs or conditions.

I left Anatole because George had told me not to stay away more than a few hours. It had been the most wonderful day I could remember, and I decided right then that I belonged on West 72nd Street. Although I never saw Anatole again, I never forgot his gentle laugh.

When I left, the men who owned the stores came outside and waved at me as though I were someone special. It is the people who elected me, the people of 72nd Street who made me enchanted. Not only Anatole, but Socrates, owner of the Oedipus luncheonette, the Ping-Pong instructor Jean Louis, an old man I played Scrabble with, the men standing on corners half asleep with drugs, the proprietors of small grocery stores, the Argentinian pianist who sells records, the owner of Le Petit Four, and many, many others.

That evening, after George and I had sex as we had every evening at 10 P.M., I asked him if we might move further downtown. Fortunately I did not mention the exact street. It is my street and he might have gone and set fire to the stores or killed Anatole. His response was to have one of his rages. Sex has nothing to do with preventing rages—at least in George—or helping anything for more than a second. I wonder who started the rumor about relationships and marriages falling apart because of sex. It isn't true. George and I never had a sexual problem. He was knowledgeable and unselfish with sex—only with that. Some of the craziest, sickest, most destructive men I have known have been excellent lovers. Problems rarely come from sex unless someone isn't interested or has too many rules. George's rules were about other things. But after finding my true kingdom I didn't care so much about George's dismissals, about his rages, or even about not being able to laugh. If I hadn't been so deeply in love with George and his beard I might have realized that his changes were permanent. I waited for George to improve and hoped that Doctor Clufftrain did not want George all to himself.

Doctor Clufftrain did want George all to himself. After George got his doctorate I was asked to leave. I moved immediately to my 72nd Street. One day I heard that George, upon the advice of Doctor Clufftrain, had shaved off his beard and was selling shoes in a store near the good doctor's office.

—

It is becoming too hard for me and I write faster and faster but soon I may explode. All kinds of orange flowers are growing out of my arms and nipples and toes and belly. They are tickling me. I am singing loudly, a beautiful contralto it sounds like, and they are demanding my appearance. The streets are lonely, need my laughter and jewels and friendship. I cannot read my notes and cards any longer. They make no sense. I am glowing almost feverishly and need to express my joy, the joy that is cracking out of every pore or petal or cell and is in the bloodstream, veins, arteries down to the tiniest capillary. And it goes from me into the tables and chairs, and atoms fly around the room. Those colored atoms are also full of joy. It isn't right to sit at a typewriter inhibiting the radiance. Radiance needs people and activity. What are the limits? I must try to remember. Yes, no stealing and no going about undressed. I wonder if being covered with flowers constitutes nudity? I mustn't loiter.

I was taken away one night of Radiance 3 for dancing at dawn in Riverside Park. The boats were splashing and from one yacht window a red light shone for me. I knew. The air was misty and felt warm to my skin and I heard the sweetest music and couldn't stop whirling, like those mad dervishes or cossacks or bullfighters, thinking I was like Isadora Duncan and my body was beautiful and free. I was wearing a long flowered skirt with nothing on top, not for exhibitionism—I thought I had thin veils hanging over my breasts. From yacht windows they were applauding me. More lanterns were hung and candles were held as people awoke and came from their boats to watch Salomé. The park was a blazing glory. Nothing like it had ever been seen before with all those magic lights shining in the mist and those boats rocking.

My dance was danced not only for myself but for all of life, all living things and for the sick to make them better, like the Indians do, and to heal the souls of my people and to make everyone's wishes come true. Such happiness I experienced, I wish everyone could. No passive waiting for divine revelations or bliss or a white light. Yoga is too still for me, oppressive. Radiance can never be contained because of being a generous thing. The body was made to move and so much had I sat frozen in corners that I wanted to dance. Then why was it illegal?

Why did they call it insanity and jab that needle into my buttocks so I couldn't dance even if I wanted to? But I do remember that night. Most things are hazy and blurred and far away, but the things that were really true and expressive of radiance stay in my brain in spite of the drugs or anything.

Now is another time—afternoon. Whatever the consequences I must move, must float, must greet and sing and leave this room.

Perhaps if I put a sheet over me I cannot be arrested. I will tie it sari fashion and put on all my jewels and go outside. Dangerous or not it cannot be helped. I am too happy, too full of the hot sun in my veins, too full of leafy candles and butterflies in my head to stay here and crack the flowers of my hands. Maybe this denial is wrong anyhow, this forcing myself to think coherently and dwell upon the past. It is a compromise which I have never been good at. Even when I began painting the backgrounds black and outlining the features. I felt guilty. It was wrong, a lie like this, like not being what I am supposed to be. I may never have the radiance again. Without Thorazine I may be destroying my own precious condition, changing my chemistry and all the while going back and forth.

—

They were so happy to see me, had missed me on the corner of Columbus where I often stop in my usual condition for coffee or an orangeade. I like the balance—at the foot of the street is Orange Julius and here at the head is an ordinary old-fashioned orangeade counter which serves watery coffee. It is usually frequented by construction men, carpenters, janitors, supers, and local proprietors.

The men thought I looked regal in my draped sheet tied sari style with glittering rhinestone pins stuck into it. From my earlobes hung my heaviest earrings in contrast to my bare feet. My hair was hanging kinky and matted from the heat, and lots of blusher rouge brightened my eyes which were heavily outlined in black so that they sparkled. Sean O'Reilly talked to me about Irish literature, the war in Belfast, and the romantic castles and beaches of Ireland. He is a construction worker—a plasterer to be exact—wearing plaster-covered pants, dusty boots, and a fly pinned together with a large safety pin. He has intelligent blue eyes and a face with patches of red from drink.

I've never spoken to Sean O'Reilly before and the waiter and other men at the counter seemed happy to see me so voluble because I usually sit there without even looking up, just reading my letters. I feel better reading my mail at the counter, in case there is anything humiliating, so I go downstairs at exactly 1:00 after the oriental mailman has completed his sorting. This stand is not frequented by the richer people who live between Central Park West and Columbus, only by the workers and Puerto Ricans, blacks, Irish, and others who live along Columbus or between Broadway and Columbus. Homosexual men don't like it there.

Sean O'Reilly was delighted with the lilt in my voice and with my singing. All the men laughed and clapped as though we were in a pub in Ireland and I wasn't thinking of arrests but of the flowers over me and how nice it was for the men to enjoy my singing. Then I began to tell Sean in a loud voice about my joy in the people who plaster walls so white with spatulas and about how I would like to do that—climb up high on a scaffold and wash windows or shimmy up the edge of a building and lay bricks one by one. This speech made them clap and cheer. I sat on the counter like a café singer with my legs crossed and my head thrown back singing and sipping orangeade. No one stopped me, only passersby stared or laughed while Sean was looking into my eyes with his silvery look wanting to come up before he went back to work. But just then some man was walking past calling my name, and it got confusing because I was no longer with Sean but with him or someone else, and I can't remember what my exact relationship was or whether he then came up here or whether Sean did with his beautiful Irish brogue and safety pin. Maybe no one did. After all the sun was shining out there. Yet it seems that someone did and that I finally slept because I haven't since it began.

I woke up wearing the white sheet and having some scratches from the rhinestone pins, and I was feeling sorry that I had rolled over smothering the pretty goldenrods but they can grow back. Sean is going to meet me there tomorrow so he can watch me dance in the park near the yachts. He laughed with his blue eyes and promised. I am so glad I spilled so much joy in that place where people are usually sullen and afraid to look at anyone. Some of my time is unaccounted for. Hours are lost when I am not here and sometimes when I am. So are dreams. But it has changed.

The first radiance was a total eclipse except for that light feeling of well-being, like being loved. That was some time after I had visited Doctor Clufftrain with George. It began on a bus to 72nd Street on about my third visit. All I remember is a sudden feeling of loving and being loved, all tender and directed everywhere. The bus expanded and contracted with myself laughing and others catching it and then wandering. The next thing I knew is that I was on a ward in Bellevue and George was putting on an act of being concerned. He impressed those young medical students and interns, but it never stopped him from telling me that he didn't want me around anymore, or plotting against me with Doctor Clufftrain. Later he told me about the shameful things I had done, the drunk men I had brought to his apartment, my startling half-nude dances, and the total lack of cohesion in my thoughts. George said it was just a magnification of my usual sloppy thinking and that he had called an ambulance after breaking some of his own fingers. He tried to make me think I had been insane. I don't know if he made up any of it, especially the lewd things, but at the time I was upset about not remembering.

After that, he and Doctor Clufftrain had a lot of evidence against me and that made George able to work very hard on his dissertation.

It no longer frightens me not to remember certain nights or hours or to find a drug addict or other stranger in my bed. I accept it and hope to remember more and not to do anything obscene.

—

Each radiance is different. This one is like ocean waves. It is uneven. Sometimes I am almost the same as I was before and other times I am drowned. It reminds me of Dr. Jekyll taking the magic chemical and becoming elated and without his puritanical morality and remembering partly what he did and wanting to do it again. But it isn't the same. No one has ever photographed me during an "attack," but I suspect that I look like a saint in ecstasy.

My aim is to be able to control the radiance completely, to make it flood over me or retreat completely at will. This might not be its nature but perhaps by my ninth I will be able to. I already have a little control. I can remember some of the things I do very clearly. I remembered about talking with Sean O'Reilly at the counter. I just don't remember what happened during the rest of the day. But the most important thing is I have not yet been taken away.

—

For several months BTR—before this radiance—I was seeing and sleeping with a man whom I met in the Greek luncheonette, the Oedipus, on the corner of 72nd Street. He lives in the Mayfair Towers next to the Dakota but not facing Central Park. Someday I will live in the Dakota. I have met many men in the Oedipus luncheonette beginning with Anatole. It is largely a matter of persistence and of looking unconscious deliberately. For example, when I saw Alan I liked his beard although it wasn't nearly as long as George's beard. His eyes were grayish-blue and looked intelligent and he had well-shaped hands. I did not like his scarab pinky ring or his suit. In general I don't like it when a man is wearing a suit which has the two parts matching like a set and which is perfectly clean. I prefer men to make errors and to be unconscious or vague about attire. I am not of the school that believes that the human male is like the male birds and should look fancier than the woman. Also, despite the current controversy, I prefer that the man pay for me and open doors and even send flowers. Of course flowers can mean nothing at all. Someone can belong to a flower-sending club or do it so you can't be angry. Of course women should have the vote. Otherwise, despite its problems, I am content that a man think he is the aggressor, make the phone calls, and pay for taxicabs. This is shocking to some people who get angry if a man opens a door or looks at their breasts. In general I favor biology. I have my own prejudices just as men do. I prefer a lot of hair on a man's chest and that he not exhibit it by opening his shirt.

Alan was preoccupied with his food as men are. He was eating a pie. Men tend to think that they owe it to themselves to eat a pie whenever they have the opportunity. It was easy for me to slip onto the turning chair beside him without any suspicion being aroused. Of course the Greek waiters have seen me do this before so maybe they are on to it. My breasts were showing through which is always a good way to meet a man whether or not you like it or are liberated. I just tapped his suit and asked him to pass the sugar and then dropped the sugar. It takes no more than that to meet someone. Once you have dropped the sugar his attention is taken away from the pie and he notices your breasts.

I was sorry to find out that Alan was a lawyer although I was not surprised. The Reform Democrat lawyers abound on West 72nd Street although they do not belong there. They tend to be somewhat pompous, overly ambitious, and polygamous for its own sake. They sport motorcycles, take summer shares in the East Hamptons, and marry teachers of special education or social workers. What do you do to keep bread on the table? he asked. Such a question phrased in that way usually makes me depart. But I was feeling tolerant and forgave him because Reform Democrat lawyers don't know any better. I told him that I had no bread on my table which he thought was very amusing. Then I admitted to painting heads with black backgrounds and he became enthused. Alan collects art—at least Alan thinks he collects art. Most men who collect art collect horrible things that other men also collect. They all love Monet's *Water Lilies*. I shuddered to think what his collection might contain. I already knew: a Miro print, a brownish landscape or something with a ship, a badly done nude with her ass showing, and probably some piece of junk that he thought was contemporary abstract sculpture. I have seen many collections in men's apartments. They all love Klee and wooden sculptures of women with long breasts and hands raised upward. The impressionists are their favorite with Escher's prints coming in second. Ugh!

Alan was your usual man in many ways with the inevitable *Catch-22, Portnoy's Complaint, The Naked Lunch, The Alexandria Quartet, Lolita, Shōgun, The French Lieutenant's Woman,* and Masters and Johnson's research books on his shelves. He also had a subscription to the New York City Opera and a collection of Baroque records. This is the type of man I usually don't get along with but I try to keep an open mind. Alan was intelligent and seemed kind. In my last hospital (Radiance 6) I was told to associate with kind men. However these are difficult to recognize or to find, particularly among the employed. Many unemployed men are exceedingly sensitive and kind although they spend the days wandering through city parks and seeing free films in the museums. Alan seemed both kind and employed. There was a definite attraction between Alan and myself right there at the counter, and he paid for my coffee which some women would object to as a form of patronization but which I thought was polite and appropriate never having been brainwashed. Our relationship progressed in time. Alan was consistent which is a rare attribute in a man, as is punctuality. He could be romantic and even had a few ideas all his own.

Our main problem came from dining. I hate to dine. Alan loved to try new foods at new restaurants and to spend a lot of time with the menu. He was hurt when I ordered only one thing and no soup or appetizer. Dining drives me crazy. I cannot stand menus and making a fuss about what is to be eaten and tasting each other's food. It was the highlight of Alan's life. I don't like the din of voices in a restaurant or the lighting or the politeness of the waiters or waiting for the food. It never works out. I either get sick from the food or vertigo from the entire atmosphere. If it takes too long to decide upon a restaurant, I become faint and hypoglycemic. I have fainted in many restaurants and left full plates of food and lost my appetite from the entire ceremony. Alan was as irritated by my behavior in restaurants as I was by his. There is nothing to talk about in a restaurant except the food.

The danger of being silent was that Alan would begin to look at the women seated at different tables. Alan began to like tall Nordic blondes particularly because I am small and dark and regal like a Princess must be—at least in my realm. I have often wondered why people like to go in pairs to a restaurant that is full of other pairs. It reminds me of an orgy, seems to be built around the same principles. There must be some particular pleasure in public digestion that I cannot feel. Alan persisted. My life became a nightmare of restaurants with enormous menus and tall blonde women. Secretly Alan thought I was a dwarf although he never said it. I had to depend upon the compliments of other men to reassure myself. This made our relationship pathetic.

I had given up living with men after George, so after dining and sex Alan would walk me across the street. I would go upstairs, dress again, and appear in O'Toole's Saloon which is always full of admiring men. One of the small unemployed men drinking beer at the bar would tell me how beautiful I was. In O'Toole's, I am definitely recognized for what I am. The bartenders know who I am but never presume to chat with me or to look at my breasts. They have great respect for my position in the neighborhood. Alan never complimented my appearance even during vigorous copulation, so I was forced to acquire a group of late-evening admirers. I have no idea why Alan kept seeing me. He needed a tall blonde dining companion more than anything else. I continued with it because I was trying to like someone who was unlike George. Alan was consistent, not overtly cruel, and had money for taxicabs so we didn't have to search on foot for all those restaurants.

I never leave 72nd Street except in a car or a taxicab. Traveling any other way makes me anxious, subject to secretions of epinephrine, heart palpitations, loss of color, and vertigo. I feel perfectly well where I reign, where I control the streets and lend my personality to the establishments.

I don't like to dine and hate crowds. I only like empty theaters, all-night diners, sex, and conversations. Most men don't converse. That is why they have to keep doing things, I guess, like eating or jogging. Most conversation occurs right at the beginning when each one is telling the other whether or not he or she has been married, the kinds of movies they prefer, what they do, where they used to live, date of birth, and other useless information. It makes them think they are not strangers. For example, I told Alan that I had lived with George for a period of three years during which time I ceased to laugh, sing, or speak and that George's psychiatrist was president of the Society to Preserve Roots by which is meant roots of trees, roots of teeth, and anything else you can think of. Alan expressed compassion implying that with him I would be able to sing and laugh and say whatever I wished. However, there was nothing to laugh about and no reason to sing. I told Alan that I had gone to art school and had been married to Adolphe, a man who painted sinks full of dirty dishes and garbage cans full of garbage—all with simple shapes and a lot of sweet pinks and fuchsia—on enormous canvases. He had a nervous breakdown because he painted a large traffic light thinking it to be his work of genius and another student coincidently painted a traffic light which was better than his. Adolphe then slashed his own painting and the painting of the other student and sat in a corner shaking with rage. I sat in another corner watching him and also shook. We almost starved. He finally went into a mental institution in Chicago. I followed and worked in a restaurant frequented by people of the Chicago underworld. When he came out he admitted that he couldn't love anyone and was not interested in sex. I had suspected this already but was too idealistic to mention it at the time. My husband didn't paint anymore but pasted spools of thread in huge towers and became quite well-known in the Chicago art world.

Alan was shocked at this story and promised to show me that there was love and devotion in the world. Nothing went on in-between, in all the months that followed, except sex and dining and going to the New York City Opera. There was talking again at the end when everything that should have been said tumbled out in madness.

Alan, you make me feel ugly like a dwarf with your admiration of tall Nordic blondes with huge breasts. That's only human nature, Alan replied. You do not understand my royal blood. He laughed. I don't know what you want and I've tried to give you everything and to understand your peculiar behavior in restaurants. You never express your feelings and thus prevent me from expressing mine. That's not fair, I just don't happen to have fears, doubts, or conflicts like you do; you are only interested in what is going on in your head rather than what is happening in the world. Alan, I think you are afraid to know what you fear or doubt and that's why the world of law and politics obsesses you. True, the economy and politics are beyond petty personal concern not like your paintings which are involuted and suffocating, and you should develop a sense of the outer world and paint landscapes. Explore the universe. It is you who need to explore; exploration is not only external like tasting food. Look, if what I have to give is insufficient, then why do you continue to see me? It is you who continue to see me out of laziness. You're too lazy to go out and find a tall blonde. You take tall blondes too seriously, and I stayed because I care for you. Your indifference is infuriating, your easygoing facade, love of eating. Where are you hiding? I enjoy the better things of life, and most women would like those restaurants; you just like to dwell upon yourself, and you don't really see anyone else clearly despite your alleged sensitivity. How dare you say that. You're so insensitive that you deserve a tall Nordic blonde who will gladly love you for your money and eat twice as much as you do, and I hope you find her.

There were days of talking at the end and days of yelling and crying and coming together and parting, throwing things and throwing up and going to bed. And all this because there had been no talking in the middle.

I tried to remember it next time—to make things clear at the outset—that I hate to dine and to end the relationship then and there before I suffered through all those menus and silences and overdoses of monosodium glutamate and false pretenses. But I failed.

I missed Alan's consistency and his flowers, and his occasional moods of romance. Otherwise there was nothing to miss.

—

Last night it ebbed, just so I knew everything that was going on and had hands of flesh and bone though light and graceful—hands that did not move clumsily like most. I could feel each part of my body, yet nothing contracted or felt heavy or tense. In that condition, surprised and pleased at this perfect control and better able to appreciate the benefits, I dressed knowing that my dress was correct if not the same as usual. Instead of going without a top as I did when I danced near the yachts, I lifted my long golden print skirt above my breasts, not feeling the cut of the elastic. Around my waist I wound several ordinary chiffon scarves and some that I bought during this or another radiance which cost only forty-nine cents and are covered with sequins or other shiny matter. I brushed my hair out as straight as it would go and, not satisfied with its gleam, shined it with vaseline. The result was amazing. My hair shone like a black mirror. On my eyelids were the colors of the rainbow and the black line around my eyes extended inches beyond, slanting upward. A red dot, Indian style, was in the center of my forehead, and a veil covered the bottom of my face. The effect was bewitching. It isn't how I usually dress on 72nd Street, but it was nothing I cannot remember doing slowly and carefully.

Then I floated outside into my kingdom knowing that no one would recognize me. The short men of 72nd Street all followed me singing and playing stringed instruments. Some of them ran out of O'Toole's Saloon to watch as I danced and twirled down the street. The moon had a reddish tint to it and there were blue stars everywhere. Odors of spicy food drifted toward me from the Japanese restaurants and from Hector's Cuban Restaurant and from all the garbage pails along Columbus Avenue. Salt spray jumped from the river several blocks away.

Alone I sat at a table in Gladstone's Bar, outside, where the walls are glass and everyone passing could see me. I knew that a handsome stranger would eventually come along. Meanwhile I winked at the men with their wives or dates who turned to look at me. I rolled my golden-brown, almond-shaped eyes and laughed warmly from beneath my veil. It was not like flirting with married men or taking someone away because I was in another realm. In this universe it would have been totally unnatural if all men did not stare at me with reverence and desire. I knew that those plain-looking women with blonde hair and grotesque breasts understood that I was beyond and above those men who sat beside them covertly glancing in my direction. In fact the women bowed their heads in solemn recognition of my divinity.

It was a feeling of small bells ringing and showers of light, something smooth and gentle proven by the fact that I was able to sit still gazing quietly. More often radiance causes me to be perpetually moving and dancing quite rapidly covering miles of space in no time. I told the waiter that I was waiting for someone. He is dark-haired with a white turban and a black moustache, carrying a bouquet of gardenias and dressed in a scarlet coat, I whispered in a strange mixture of accents. And when he passed by I ran outside and brought him to my table. He didn't ask me anything or resist but followed gladly. He staggered a little from the excitement and smelled of rich purple vineyards. I took a white chiffon scarf from around my waist and wound it gently around his head. There it sat. All this was done with such grace and so naturally that the man waited silently neither afraid nor suspicious—just silently gazing into my hypnotic eyes. With the intuition of an Arabian princess, I had chosen a true Arab. He said some words and ordered drinks. The words were, my name is Kulack and I am a wine merchant from Bagdad. His shirt was pure silk and his jacket was brocade. I have journeyed here to meet you and to give you my wealth and wine cellars, he said kissing my hand. Everything he said was perfect, romantic, and exotic.

Gladstone's is not normally an exotic bar. It has infiltrated from another Gladstone's on the east side of the park on 77th Street. It has little tables with red checkered cloths and no candles. Inside harsh old rock music revived is played loudly, and habitual drunkards stand at the bar. Neighborhood people sit at the tables drinking beer and eating hamburgers. Alan and I used to go into Gladstone's for hamburgers on the rare occasions when we did not dine out formally. But that Gladstone's and the one I sat in last night are not the same.

There were candles on the tables and waiters sitting on cushions playing sitars. Kulack, I must dance, I said and began my dance of the seven veils. Kulack remarked that the floor was too small. He took some silver coins from a jeweled bag and threw them on the floor and we went out into the mysterious night. He begged to see my face but I told him that it was forbidden. We walked two doors south of the orangeade stand until we reached a black door. He pulled open the door to what used to be a Haitian restaurant specializing in mediocre jazz. Now it was a mystery. Down these stairs, I said in an urgent whisper to Kulack who staggered but obeyed.

There in the violet-lit basement sat a group of enchanted Arabs playing American instruments. The drummer was dark and fat and of royal extraction. A young, bearded, religious man played an electric piano and a tall one—a majestic freak of Arabia—was bending his knees squeezing all of his breath into a horn. The electric bass had a look of distracted wisdom. He knew more than the others. I judged him to be the silent leader who communicated his musical intentions. The flutist was not a man but a puppet with a strange orange wig and costume of plaid pants and sneakers. He was strung like a marionette. The bass made him move and play exquisitely. I want him, I said to Kulack, pointing to the flutist. He grew stern and jealous as men are apt to be, particularly men from Bagdad. Kulack began to look sinister. He's only a toy, I said. I want him. Kulack took a drink and laughed and promised to buy him for me. I was sending my thoughts which were fluid and musical to the electric bass player who must have recognized Kulack. Therefore he acknowledged nothing but ordered a female marionette to come out and sing. She is poorly made, I told Kulack who looked at me with adoration while perspiration trickled from his brow and onto his jeweled cape.

Only a few couples were dancing. At a signal from the electric bass who never blinked an eye, I got up and began. Kulack jumped up to dance with me. But although he danced nearby, I danced alone—a gesture of homage to the musicians. I did a modified belly dance which on an ordinary night I wouldn't have been supple enough to have done. Radiance be blessed, I was able to think—an amazing thought and one like a prayer of thanks as my body performed intricate miracles that made Kulack and all the other players fall further in love with me. My joy and beauty spread itself everywhere. More people danced and soon the entire basement was in motion. At this point waves flowed everywhere and I remember little—only exquisite musical sounds and Kulack's strong dark arms and his white turban. I smelled aromatic nut-flavored oil.

This morning when I awoke I discovered a note from someone. It read: You were very entertaining, must take the children to the beach this morning, will call you, James Kulack. I keep reading it but it makes no sense. What beach and whose children are they? Who is this James Kulack? It puzzles and amuses me rather than being anything of great importance as it might be at another time. But at another time I would not have met a turbaned Arab named Kulack who treated me with such distinction. During my other "attacks" I have not remembered as much, although I never forgot everything except during the first and second. So I must conclude that they are changing—are building up slowly or that each one is different.

I like remembering and knowing. Otherwise it is almost as though it never happened. I prefer to collect my visions. Last night

I tasted my radiance without having to control it and then at the very end it was eclipsed. But I am safe, and Kulack must have taken care that the Bagdad police did not seize and arrest me.

—

I am not one of those rulers who is never seen on the streets mingling with the common people. Issues concern me such as the welfare and privacy of my residents. It disturbs me to see the bicycle lane on Central Park West. It makes travel from East to West and from West to East too easy. Mingling, interaction, and even intermarriage result. Values become corrupted and some of the good people leave. I hope to close up this exit once and for all—not only to cars but to bicycles. There is no need to visit the Eastside at all. There are doctors and psychiatrists on the West. And some day I will set up a program to import more urologists, cardiologists, and radiologists. There are hospitals on the Westside but not on West 72nd Street. We need one badly in this great realm.

I think of things like this when I make my two daily tours. The first begins at 1:00 in the afternoon when I go downstairs to collect my mail. Sometimes I miss this tour because I am trapped in the elevator. This happens periodically, the elevator being hopeless, obsolete, and dangerous. At midnight I make my second tour entering most of the bars, restaurants, and coffee shops. It gives people a feeling of reassurance to see me up and about making mental notes and checking up on the workings of the neighborhood. My interest in each shopkeeper, waiter, bartender, bricklayer, and superintendent is obvious to all. They bask in my care and await my daily appearances.

—

Auriel was standing in front of Saul the Tailor's dressed in a black velvet jacket and plum-colored velvet pants. His hair was long and blonde. Fluttering doves appeared and disappeared from inside his coatsleeves. I fixed the coat and it was no easy task, no indeed, Saul, the tailor, whispered proudly to the people gathered around Auriel. The people of 72nd Street were not interested in who made the coat but in Auriel's exquisite performance. The doves flew up in the air or perched on Auriel's head and then, as if by some mysterious prompting, they vanished. Many eyes were seen looking for them up in the sky, to the right or left. With a faint smile perpetually on his lips, Auriel found the doves up his sleeve. The crowd stared at him in amazement and applauded.

He was tall and strangely built. Narrow shoulders were hunched up to his ears and thrust forward, and his legs turned inward. Long white toes stuck out of black leather sandals. Their pointed toenails curved toward the ground. Auriel's eyes were half-closed in a sort of ecstasy. People gave him money that he collected in a bag made of tapestry beginning to unravel at the top.

Something about this man both fascinated and repelled me. His cheeks were slightly rouged, and he had silver enamel on his fingernails. A silver star was drawn on his forehead. Underneath the black velvet jacket he wore a satin shirt with tan and pink flowers painted on a dark background.

It was to this man, Auriel, an illusionist, that I told the truth.

As if by mutual agreement, I remained while the doves were placed gently inside a cage that had been lying on the pavement. Auriel bowed to the people as they slowly dispersed. Then he and I began to walk toward Broadway. I am Auriel, he said in a very soft voice. I am Princess Esmeralda of West 72nd Street, I answered, realizing that it was the first time I had said this name to anyone or even spoken it aloud. My real name, Ellen, the one given to me by my mother and the one I am known by and use to sign checks with, is not my true name.

Esmeralda or Princess Esmeralda came to me early, perhaps on my first or second voyage to 72nd Street while I was still living with George. I don't know why this name came to me—its exact origin is unimportant. But that it is my inner name is a simple fact. Something about Auriel called forth the truth from me about this and about all things. As I had known intuitively, my name and title seemed perfectly natural to him. It was an important day in my life—the day I met Auriel. It was a month after the sixth radiance. It was after I was dining with Alan and somehow overlaps the end of Alan. Yet I am not exactly certain unless there is a gap somewhere in time. For how is it possible that I could have been with Alan the lawyer and Auriel the illusionist at the same time? And yet it is—days being endless and plentiful and even bountiful sometimes.

We walked and I showed him each landmark of my realm. Finally we came to the end and had something to eat at The Copper Hatch which is a café that has gone through several phases. Still, it is basically unchanged, with a small bar inside and tables several steps down from the outside area which is surrounded by glass panels. The glass panels used to be absent and the tables were right on the street, but for winter use and heating panels became necessary. My impression at the time was that Auriel was asexual or homosexual or sexual in some way other than the ordinary. People stared at him, but he appeared not to notice. I love wigs, he said laughing a child's laugh. Then he told me to close my eyes. When I opened them, Auriel had short brown hair and looked quite different. Changes frighten me, I said, and he looked unhappy and asked if he should put the blonde wig on again. He held it up and we both laughed. Auriel told me that he liked to vary his appearance and had many expensive wigs of all styles and that I could choose the one I preferred him to wear except when he was performing. He offered to go without one. I began to cry. It cannot be explained except to say that I had been waiting for someone to talk to for a long time and that no one had understood before. When I cried, Auriel held my hand inside his. It was a soft hand, not to my immediate liking with its silver nail decoration, but there are many things in the world to adapt to and prejudices to overcome. I love you, Auriel said, and then asked if he should not have said it. If it is true, then there is no special time to say it, I answered. Then I asked him why. Because you are the most beautiful person in the world, he said. I am that if you believe it, I answered.

I was aware of the unworldly quality to our speech and worried about where we could go from this lofty beginning, and what we could be to each other in reality. I did not think about this too carefully, but what was disturbing me, I know now, is the schism that has always been inside me. Auriel was simple and pure and therefore could only see and love the spiritual and sweet Princess Esmeralda. Inside there also lived Ellen with great anger, a sense of the world of material necessity, economics, politics, and growth. Ellen was always looking for a man suitable to be her husband. Auriel questioned nothing, was content to look at me and believe that I, too, was simple and unquestioning. I told him about the radiance. He thought it was something I should be proud of and not consider an illness. I am made of white light, he said seriously. All things are, he added.

That was my first meeting with Auriel. I knew better than to ask him where he lived or how. It was enough then that Auriel loved Princess Esmeralda of 72nd Street and her radiance. He walked me to my apartment building with the broken elevator, kissed my cheek, and said that he had to take the doves home to be fed.

Auriel had the idea of putting on a huge production with his doves while a chorus narrated the story of the false creation which is matter on this plane. Gradually the stage would become brighter as the eternal plane of existence was reached. Then the doves would fly against a sky that was also white and he, Auriel, would disintegrate into white light as would everything. Then the people would realize the truth as spoken to Auriel personally by Guru Maharaj-goo who came from India to save the world. However, when I asked Auriel when this performance would take place, he only said that there was no hurry and that the time would be revealed.

I was deeply in love with Auriel and tried to retain, when with him, the sweet trusting nature of Princess Esmeralda. He wanted to please her, would do anything to protect her. But constant exposure to Auriel made her strangely weary. Ellen was annoyed because all of Auriel's ideas were taken from the Maharaj-goo. He stole opinions uncritically from magazine articles and repeated them as absolute truth. And then he took thoughts and opinions from Ellen, asked her how he should behave and what he should do or say. Princess Esmeralda was honored by the love of Auriel. She thought he was a magnificent prince. Ellen suspected that nothing lay beneath the frail identity of makeup and wigs. She felt like he was draining her. Esmeralda often lay in bed inert, and Auriel went out and did the shopping, went for walks alone, and performed on street corners. He expressed concern at her pallor and weakness. He thought she should see the Maharaj-goo. Ellen began to hate the Maharaj-goo.

When Auriel made love with Esmeralda, it was with reluctance and inevitable self-chastisement. He claimed to be waiting for the time when he would no longer be trapped on the physical plane which was false. This was too much not only for Ellen but for Princess Esmeralda, particularly since Auriel, seeming to be pure and inexperienced, devised sinister and decadent aspects to their lovemaking. Sometimes he put a thin black stocking over his face or had them both wear identical brassieres made of silver mesh or pasted feathers all over his body from head to toe. Endless were these varieties. In this area Auriel's creativity and personality were quite vivid. It excited him to paint his nipples, which were very sensitive, a deep green color. He painted hers red or turned them into twin anemones or blue fish. After a while this sexual experimentation and ornamentation was their main activity. Esmeralda was too weak to get out of bed, and Auriel, beneath his childlike laughter and spirituality, was a master of sensuality. I think I am not sick but that you drain my strength, she told Auriel at last. He looked depressed and said it had happened before—that he had that effect upon women and didn't know why. He then mentioned that she had lost much of her sweetness and always wanted to quarrel. What he, Auriel, wanted was serenity. She complained that he could not accept anger or express it. He tried to please her by expressing anger. First it was contrived. Then he became violent, screamed in a falsetto, and cracked mirrors, vases, and windowpanes with a hammer.

He began to wander away and was absent when she needed him. She couldn't reach him since he had no address. Upon intense, hysterical questioning Auriel confessed that he lived with a woman most of the time—in her apartment. She had also been beautiful. At times he lived with others. He said that his love for her, Princess Esmeralda, had not been connected in any way with these women and that he had planned to rid himself of everyone else—that was before she had begun to ask pointed questions, mock his religion, and have tantrums. Then she had become a part of the One Great Love and no longer its very essence as she had been at first. The other women were also part of the One Great Love.

After Auriel left she received many hysterical phone calls from women asking if he were there. I have not seen Auriel for weeks, she replied. Sometimes Esmeralda waited for him in front of Saul the Tailor's. Ellen objected. She thought that Auriel was not very bright, promiscuous, self-centered, and a fake.

—

That is what happens to precious feelings when they are questioned. My Prince Auriel with the white doves and exquisite fingers used to bring me gifts, produce flowers from emptiness, and blow gigantic rainbow bubbles on my breasts. And all I did was to criticize him for not having any plans or ideas of his own, for not having a place where I could reach him. And then I raged against the white light and its negation of simple reality.

Sometime before this Radiance 7, sometime before or after Alan and I were arguing, I received a phone call from a woman who was screaming and crying. It is your fault, she said. Auriel strangled his doves and then hung himself right in my apartment. I am the only one who loved him and understood him but he left a note saying: I love Princess Esmeralda.

I want my Auriel back, I thought. I would try to understand and never crush his pitiful identity. I felt as evil as those who arrest me and those who put Stelazine into my veins. I destroyed Auriel. Now no one will know my real name.

I envisioned Auriel with a faint smile on his lips choosing his favorite wig, rouging his cheeks, and stepping into the noose he had learned to prepare. Auriel is choking, gasping for breath. His arms reach instinctively to the rope to untie it, but he knows he will soon be released to that plane he is waiting for. I couldn't stand to think of it then before this seventh radiance. And at the same time Alan, knowing nothing of Auriel or Auriel's death, had finally decided to express his feelings as I had often requested. Too late Alan was telling me of his doubts and fears. Too late—after I had loved Auriel and didn't care what Alan felt—even that Alan had hidden from himself the knowledge that he loved me. He had tried to make me seem too unattractive to love by comparing me with tall blondes and others who were mountain climbers, prima ballerinas, gourmet cooks, deep sea divers, and who possessed perfect teeth.

Men are always late with their love. I only loved Auriel and felt as though I had murdered him with a rope. I told Alan to go away and Alan did. Men do go away when you tell them to, quite swiftly with never a backward glance, as though you had issued an edict in a state of irrevocable sanity and wisdom.

It occurred to me during this pre-radiant state, even while somewhat despondently attending to my kingdom, that Auriel's death might be a lie made up by the woman who had screamed, or that the voice might have been that of Auriel himself. Auriel could change his voice from bass to baritone to soprano. Unfortunately I did not know the address of that screaming woman nor any other of Auriel's addresses. I did not even know the whereabouts of Guru Maharaj-goo and his followers. I called *The New York Times* and asked if a man had strangled his doves and himself. They knew nothing about it. The city morgue informed me that there was no body in recent months tagged Auriel. If I wished to, I could come down and identify some unclaimed corpses, one of which might be Auriel. I declined, preferring to leave open all kinds of possibilities. Sometime Auriel might announce his great performance and then I could go and witness the living Auriel and claim him. But would he want me? I love him and smile as pictures of Auriel in his long blonde wig and stocking mask pass through my brain.

Despite my depression about Auriel's murder or suicide, I resolved to give my attention to 72nd Street.

It was at this time—a bad time—that my ex-husband Adolphe, whom I had last seen ten years ago at his exhibition of spools in Chicago, happened to come to New York City.

—

My ex-husband Adolphe called to speak about his work. He informed me that a great art gallery on Madison Avenue wanted to give him a one-man show. It had grown from small spools pasted together to enormous ones combined—growing like straight or tilting castles. Each work had a real traffic light at the top. He was thrilled with his achievement and forthcoming show. It was the culmination of more than ten years of driving himself and several wives insane, losing all his hair and most of his eyesight. More than anything else he wanted to show me his work. I called Melita immediately to hear what she thought. Melita is the only person besides Peter who knew me when I had a husband in Philadelphia and Chicago. Melita was jealous because her plums have never been exhibited except at public outdoor shows and in the windows of a few suburban stores. She was also worried about the effect of this news upon Peter who was very competitive. I sensed that Melita did not trust me because of my attacks of radiance and that she found it difficult to understand what Peter was doing on 72nd Street. I assured Melita once again that I did not know and had no feeling for him except pure friendship. I told her that I would appreciate it if she, Melita, or both Melita and Peter could stay with me on that day when my ex-husband would be coming to get my reaction to his colossal work—after ten years. It is too much for me, Melita, with Auriel's death and Alan expressing his feelings. Who is Auriel? Melita asked and I told her that he was a dead man whom I loved.

Melita was not getting along with Peter at all. He caught her painting a huge plum and had been drinking ever since. He had not returned to teach his art history courses on light and structure in Vermeer's paintings. I, myself, cannot help getting angry at the thought of Melita painting a plum. I can understand Peter's reaction as it is something no one could live with. But I had to give her a bribe. Melita will never do anything for anyone without a bribe. And so I promised to have many canvases and many plums ready for her when she arrived.

—

The day before Melita was to arrive, which was a day or two before my ex-husband was coming, I was stricken by pangs of conscience, confusion, and panic. I went so far as to call Doctor Clufftrain and ask for a consultation. He was eager to see me when I assured him that I no longer had any interest in George. That I went to consult Doctor Clufftrain is the only definite evidence I have that something is wrong with me and always has been.

I had no intention of seeing George, but I happened to glance inside a men's shoe store on the way to Doctor Clufftrain's office—a block away to be exact—and there was George. He was beardless, obese, and bending over someone's feet. Unfortunately he saw me and came running after me. I have never been so happy, said George, bearing no resemblance to the George who had taught classes in the Communist Manifesto and the Russian Revolution. Nor did he seem like that George who had ordered me not to sing or laugh or speak. Why are you happy? I asked just to make conversation. George told me that the academic life was false and that he had come back to basic values—to simplicity and servitude—and that he had the honor to work close enough to Doctor Clufftrain so he could shop for him and deliver his frozen breakfasts, lunches, and dinners. I am literally at his beck and call, George said with pride. I am going to see him about some problems of my own, I said. George decided that he would take the opportunity to deliver the doctor's frozen lunch and cook it while I was in consultation. I worried about what the doctor might think seeing us together, but George assured me that Doctor Clufftrain had trust in him and would not be affected by our mutual appearance. He was only partly correct. But after a lengthy explanation to the good doctor, who turned pale and spastic when we arrived together, the good doctor understood that the meeting had been accidental. George proceeded with his duties and Doctor Clufftrain invited me inside.

He was more than cordial and thanked me for releasing George and for moving away with such grace. He then told me that his particular analytic gift was getting to the heart of a person's identity. George's identity, for example, had been a superimposed false academic identity but one that had to be worked through even to its culmination in the doctorate. George has the soul of a peasant and a born servant. You, of course, did not want to see it, but I saw it at once and have succeeded in making George what he really is. Have you noticed how happy and free of resentment he is? I had to agree although I had also noticed that George's intellect had deteriorated somewhat. I observed that he, Doctor Clufftrain, was free of his former symptoms. Except for the spasm when he saw me with George, his body was relaxed, and his head did not rock from side to side. You were only the last in a series of means to an end, he said matter-of-factly. Then the brilliant Doctor Clufftrain was silent.

I told him of Auriel's death and of the arrival of my ex-husband and of Melita. I spoke about plums, sex, and radiance. It is too complicated, too filled with conflict and impending disintegration, I said. Doctor Clufftrain laughed. You thrive on complication, he said sternly. My best advice in this matter is destruction instead of false construction. Be what thou art and then act upon it. Now go away and don't come back here. My lunch is about ready. I left, carefully weighing Doctor Clufftrain's words. I considered that an insane doctor might see things that a sane one could not. The problem was that I could not decipher his advice. Yet I felt reassured. I felt that without George, the doctor saw me clearly and that perhaps my efforts to simplify my thoughts and life were as wrong for me as putting in a black background so that the outline of the head could be seen. Maybe complication was something I had to accept and enhance. But the thing Doctor Clufftrain had not understood was that I felt no control over these events and did not know how to deal with them.

—

My concentration begins to slip despite the fact that I am sitting here. I don't know how many days or hours I have missed since it began. Never before has it been unattended and there may be danger. I remember being told that I shouldn't be alone at these times. I am a plant, a vine spreading out, crawling along, being nourished, so happy that all of my leaves are turning toward the sun. A slight warm breeze makes all my leaves quiver, and down in my roots the water tickles and gurgles, sending up colored bubbles like small burps. A thick haze spreads over all the hours and thoughts, so thoughts are not born to die but are there in a steady stream of joy—internal—probably where the small cells are that make up all the other things even turtles. My head turning on my neck or stalk if I were a flower does so naturally, in the proper rhythm, without forethought, and the smells go together. I sink into a soft mist not too hot or cold which seems to caress my skin like a great love who is a lover also and everything drifts and nothing should be stopped or segmented nor can it be because when I move everything moves with me and my voice comes from far away...

Two nights lost, two nights maybe more with only a few things remembered today—mostly drops of rain, warm and slow, then very fast hoofbeating, an apartment with reddish light from a Japanese lantern, the shower, and music. It was Schumann's *Carnival*, or that is remembered from another time and the sound was a saxophone crying. Someone was there—large, almost fat, with nice hands and words blending. No time, only an ecstasy lasting a day or two days. Only the sensation that is the opposite of anxiety or loneliness or shaking. It cannot be explained except as a reversal of the thinking and thinking with the head aching and the body moving heavily and not knowing how far. It is the opposite of effort—a funny combination of joy and peace and no matter that I don't remember more precise details. It was in someone's apartment, raining so beautifully within, and somehow I got here without bruises, and the feeling that something happened so splendid not to ever happen forever, so I would like to know who it was, but evidently I was dressed properly and he didn't drive me off to an emergency room. I know people would find this awful because time was lost and it could have been dangerous, but it seldom is dangerous and is remembered with the soul. It is like a glorious holiday with nothing to worry about. I wonder if the beautiful animals live more like this or what it would be like if everyone did.

—

I wanted to tell about Melita coming here to paint plums. But the night before she arrived I walked in my own kingdom, which I love despite its faults. I remember sitting at the bar in Gladstone's. A man drinking alone was standing his pennies, nickels, and quarters on their edges. I watched him and then I said hello or something similar. I could hear by his accent that he was from way outside—that he had selected West 72nd Street just like that after coming all the way from the Southern states. Then I went into O'Toole's. I examined the people and they all looked well. The white-haired old man who is always there was talking and drinking with another drunken regular who writes dirty stories for *Crotch Magazine.* I knew him. If you talk to him he never remembers it next time, and he is sometimes insolent from all that gin and pornography. The old man is never like that and lives forever. But I had no patience for their conversation or for the conversation of a hair stylist with beautiful hair and a dyed beard who was reading a prophecy given to him by a profound palmist. I didn't have the correct feeling for my kingdom and projected the wrong image. Some little man—the sweet small kind who doesn't work and takes some drugs but not too many anymore and sees through everything false—made the mistake of asking me to go home to bed with him.

These small men are all over my kingdom and they usually know that I am not someone you take home to bed. But I wasn't looking like the Princess of 72nd Street because of worry about tomorrow. He apologized, but I don't like it when people forget or fail to recognize my position. The bartender never forgets. He is one of the true resident angels and never stares at my tits, accepting who and what I am with keen understanding and respect. I will reward him. Some I reward and others I banish. My next door neighbor, a surly, self-centered man who had harrassed me during times of danger or radiance finally provoked me into action. I banished him from my realm. By banishing someone I mean deciding that he no longer exists. Once I decide that someone does not exist it is all over for him. I no longer say hello or glance or change my conversation or do anything when passing that I wouldn't do if indeed the space were unoccupied, even scratching my behind.

Don't think for a moment that everyone who lives in my realm deserves to be here. I never revoke a banishment. And I have certain powers. The neighbor gradually withered, declined in health and vitality, deteriorated, became destitute, and finally moved into a fleabag hotel. The cruel must be punished—an eye removed for an eye. Never forget it.

The night before Melita was scheduled to arrive I was checking everything out including the chess club, the lobsters in the window of Captain Nemo's, the cellar which used to be called Watergate Café and is slowly turning into a subterranean discotheque, and any other place that was open. But there was something detached about me—preoccupied—as though my visitors had already torn me and my realm apart.

—

Before going into the problems or chaos brought to me by my past coming to 72nd Street in the form of Melita and my ex-husband and his spools, I want to talk about The Alien who invaded my life and turned my fifth radiance into a nasty affair. This man obsesses me today as I return from great radiance into a state of simple calm. Being simply calm is odd. It is more disturbing than terror and stranger to me than radiance. I try to see it as the end of a comet's tail—a threading off of the explosion or a temporary rest. Perhaps radiance takes more energy than I am aware of and now, letting nature take its course, as they say, instead of chemotherapy, I have worn it out. This mild state is suited to The Alien. He never lived here, never belonged here, was imported by me as a lover from another realm. He could have been from another planet like Mars, Portchester, Westchester, or some part of Long Island.

I was going through a cycle of acute materialism. I have these periodically, thinking of husbands with houses, incomes, and the remote possibility of permanence and care. It is this side of me that poor Auriel could not see or ever understand. I have often kept it a secret in fact. Needing care is something you must keep carefully hidden from men so they don't panic and run. The Alien was one of those large men attracted to those needing care only to smash them up further, a common occurrence and contradiction. I see him clearly with his red beefy face, enormous belly, and skimpy gray beard without which he might have escaped my attention completely. He wore a rose in his lapel, grew and tended roses as a hobby, and got involved with interesting or peculiar women on the side. It was after my car accident which resulted in the loss of my little toe—the car seeming to center all its weight, as I crossed the street, on that teeny phalange. It has in no way impaired my walking nor left me with emotional scars or penis envy. However, a certain feeling of vulnerability due to this accident is probably what drove me into the fleshy arms of The Alien. He was a physician specializing in urology. And from the beginning Rombert wanted to help me and begged for a urine sample to put through his Mixmaster. He believed that taking apart the urine is the secret to the understanding and cure of all bodily and emotional distress.

He took it as an insult when I refused. Mistakenly, I thought urinalysis might detract from our romance. But the urine denial was what cooled his passion. He took to picking at me, to finding flaws. Rombert informed me that I was losing hair in the back, that I had an amazing number of stretch marks, and that my bite was imperfect. He was an expert at this common sport of men. I suddenly became aware of a clogged pore, of my hips which he said were asymmetrical, of my fragile bones. It was not so different from being with Alan. In fact, Rombert and Alan had a lot in common. Rombert also liked to remark about the beauty of tall stately women. I began to feel ugly. And he used to insult my kingdom, not being able to view it properly. What a pity to contemplate spending one's life on West 72nd Street, Rombert said. To some things there are no answers. Unlike Auriel, Rombert never slept over despite the distance he had to drive to reach his own territory. It was beneath him to sleep in a small apartment on West 72nd Street. I made allowances, particularly for his size and his obsessive need for ice-cold air-conditioning.

I was trying to see good in Rombert, particularly since I wanted a husband with money, and a baby. But one by one all possible virtues disappeared. Things had to be done his way; he was unreliable and broke every promise he made. Rombert thought it elegant to bring me roses from his garden, never finding out that I am not particularly fond of them. I will say that his roses were odd. Most of them were brownish-yellow and a few were orange. I wonder if urology had anything to do with the tint. I hinted about an amulet. All my life I have hinted about an amulet and have gotten boxes of cheese or roses instead. Even my beloved, deceased Auriel failed in this. Is it too much to ask? Kulack of Bagdad promised me an amulet, I remember. But that is different having occurred during the height of this seventh state of grace. No man will give me one—of that I am certain, vastly certain. It goes against the grain. If Rombert had given me an amulet, even made of urine crystals, after I lost my toe, things would be different.

In all fairness to Rombert he did offer me a urine analysis. However it wasn't an amulet—once again it was over food that problems arose. Initially I had strong feelings toward Rombert, perceived him as a well-intentioned blustering animal giving his life to treating the urinary tracts of humanity. Humanity I learned were his patients—those who came to his office on that far-off grassy planet. It was a place similar to that of Melita and Peter—a place causing arrogance because it is covered with grass instead of concrete. If someone in the street had a bladder that burst right open in front of Rombert he walked on indifferently despite the oath of Hippocrates.

A princess has her day. Thursday is mine. It is on Thursdays that I meet kind, princely men. It was on a Thursday that I lost my toe. I first met Auriel on a Thursday. And it was on Thursday that Rombert revealed the worst side of his character. Rombert was like Alan when it came to dining. Marriageable men always are. Only Alan was a better planner. With Rombert it involved hours of searching for the ultimate, the holy divine glow of a restaurant. He often had a vague idea of where it was and what it was, but never of the precise location. We searched for hours. You would have thought all this dining would please me after those years of eating rotten meatballs with George or cooking cheap stew for Adolphe. I take thee, Rombert, I used to think, and developed loving feelings in addition to conflicts, petit mal, honeymoon cystitis, and vaginismus. I love you, Ellen, because you remind me of a rose, but I have been too timid to ask for your hand, I imagined Rombert confessing and then changing into someone loving and kind. But the longer I knew Rombert the crueler he became. Some men are cruel all at once. With others it occurs after coitus. With many the hostility is lurking there all the time covered up by roses or sinister pastries.

I wore shoes equivalent to stilts knowing that, like Alan, Rombert believed that tall was superior to short. Rombert expressed it more frequently. His sons from a previous marriage were all over six-foot-three and liked to call me "shorty," a nickname they picked up from their father. Rombert was born in England and felt himself to be English which he said explained his superior nastiness, which he thought was reserve. Reserve and cruelty are two horses of a different color as they say here or in London. You are involuted and convoluted, the fault of Freud whom we have never accepted in England. Rombert said this after we had located the ultimate restaurant. It was large, brightly lit, and had emblems of approval from professional diners pasted on its doors and walls.

On this monumental Thursday night he was reading the menu which was to his satisfaction, being large and full of poor French translations. Rombert likes everything to be large including roses, women, beds, portraits, menus, dogs, cars, and diseases. I love pathology, he often muttered. The normal uninvaded body is so pedestrian, so boring, he said as he drove his gigantic car or read menus.

In all fairness to Rombert he not only loves to dine as did Alan but also loves to cook. He used to spend an entire afternoon preparing sauces and tenderizing meats while I sat outside on the lawn staring at the trees.

On this monumental Thursday, at the precise second that the main orders—veal *cordon bleu* and frog's bladder—were placed before us, I began to black out. I am blacking out, Rombert, I said. Nonsense, he replied eating the frog's bladder. I did, and when I regained consciousness, Rombert was eating and chatting at a table full of waitresses and ballerinas. His British puns evidently had them in stitches. He had forgotten about me completely as I lay between two chairs with a blanket over my head. I staggered over to him and said that I'd like to leave. Rombert did not see me or hear me for that matter. I left by myself and did not see him for several weeks. When I mentioned the incident to him sometime later he only replied that it had not occurred during office hours and that he had once offered to analyze my urine. I tried to excuse Rombert, thinking it was the English way or that the biological drive to eat conquers all or that he was terrified of fainting or any other illness such as death unless it occurred in his office. But I no longer wished to marry him. To me he is Alien, as Alien as though he were from some other universe.

He happened to arrive on a Thursday during my fifth radiance sometime after the frog's bladder incident. Seeing me so joyous, he felt it was his duty to call the police several times so that four squad cars arrived and awakened my neighbors, including the cranky, seedy banished man and the bitter widow. My apartment was full of policemen. And while I happily covered the floors with earth and planted seeds, patting them carefully and dancing upon them, Rombert tried to ingratiate himself with the police and with the bitter widow who invited him inside for stale cake. Rombert told the police that I was clinically insane and that I should be taken away for treatment, shock therapy being the most suitable, in his opinion. I shall never forgive Rombert. My entire kingdom from Central Park West to at least Broadway and 72nd Street was awakened and witnessed their Princess being put into a straitjacket—my first and last—upon medical advice from Rombert who said I might become violent in such a condition. I never have. After I was safely locked up, in Roosevelt Hospital's psychiatric ward, Rombert had a great dinner with my neighbors, bitter widow, fat spinster Patsy, seedy Sam, and a microcephalic ballerina with splayed feet.

When I returned I was marked. Certain people in my kingdom questioned my abilities and I could never be sure how many knew of this incarceration. Rombert thought it humorous to describe in detail how I thought my apartment was a garden and had planted buttons and raisins and anything else I could find. Why is that any more insane than the garden which The Alien grows in his overgrown belly?

It isn't easy to get rid of an Alien particularly when he likes to control and is awaiting another opportunity to do harm. Rombert like Peter—Melita's Peter—is always popping up when things are to his advantage, when he can display his superiority or wit. Even when he is far away his Alien influence clings to me. I almost feel smothered in rhubarb, roses, and frog's bladders. I think that Rombert will always, forever, be trying to get even with me for not giving him a sample of my urine to analyze.

—

The calm has receded, perhaps the result of internal chemicals being stirred by thoughts of Rombert. But instead of sinking my spirits rise above all this and Rombert becomes a nonsense syllable that I repeat over and over again until I fall off my chair giggling. The room takes on a greenish hue, not like the green of lawn grass but a soft blue-green, and I am filled with it. I have never taken an hallucinogenic drug and wonder if any shade of green could be as remarkable. The blue shadow is soft on my face cooling it for a moment. A musical song comes into my head and then twirls out of my scalp, and I am conscious of all this and love every bit of it, even the typewriter which is shining softly and chanting like a magical instrument producing symbols and able to copy the exact state I am in. I don't even have to worry about hitting the keys. They seem to work by themselves while I wave my hands about. An airy lighthearted mood, angelic sounds, songs, chimes meaning that there is love in the world and unity among people since their hearts are all going at approximately the same rate and all that bright red blood is flowing around and around like a merry-go-round and there are no limits to this being part of something whirling and fearless. I am so happy to be alive and want to share my happiness with everyone and need not sit here because it will write by itself being so sweet . . .

—

The green-blue comes and goes and I come and go with it not remembering except certain kisses and apartments and events in elevators, yet luck is with me. In all the aqua fog I have not been stopped by the police nor has Rombert appeared—at least as far as I know—proof being that I still have my ecstasy in varying degrees. Much too immersed in warm ocean spray to have patience for telling about that dreary week with Melita and my ex-husband and other things that happened before this magnificent Number 7. I am, in fact, flying above the salt water like a white bird. Sex, instead, occurs to me, which at all those times seemed so serious and meaningful. Now I am shaking with laughter thinking of sex and the peculiar differences in men.

I have laughed so hard that I collapsed on the floor and ate something that tasted very sweet. I didn't notice if it was an orange or grapes. I have a thousand things in the refrigerator at all times in preparation for just this event when it is so hard for me to shop or concentrate on the names of specific items. But I have managed to get back to my chair and to remember all the comical differences—comical by virtue of that difference—no man knowing how different he is and possibly thinking that each man does the same thing or something similar.

Rombert for reasons of his own, or habit, liked to hold me for a long time with my back against his big belly, underneath which grew a rather small penis. He never varied the procedure and liked to be in control taking most delight from the pleasure he gave me, withdrawing from any I might extend. At some point he would turn me over as he would turn a duck in a pan and with great pride in the length of his performance would go on and on—always above and watching my face. He had great pride in the length of time he could continue this and continued far too long and then apologized very politely for not being able to continue longer. Rombert ejaculated, but I don't think he had an orgasm unless he was being very reserved about it. Often he remarked, medical style, that my hormones were in good order and then asked, would you like a nice cup of hot tea? This was Rombert at his best, his most tender.

So different from Rombert was Auriel. Auriel, my beloved Auriel, having much spare time had passed from artistry to decadence. Auriel's body was sensitive everywhere. His was a languid approach in which everything was allowed both of us. Absolutely nothing was forbidden and no part of anyone's body neglected. He had a sluggish penis of the fluttering variety with a bluish tint contrasted to Rombert's which is pink. Because of his fluttering the actual coitus or whatever that Rombert thought most important was often absent or brief. Everything was done in the spirit of play—the different fabrics over skin, wigs, masking of his face, perforated gloves, musical accompaniment. Auriel always said, I love you, no matter how outlandish the procedure or comical, such as wearing hats and nothing else or blowing bubbles on my breasts or decorating my buttocks with silver coins or smearing chocolate syrup all over my face. There was no beginning or end. It went on like an illuminated dream or masquerade.

Unlike Auriel George was dull. He was drawn to his old couch, liked to huddle with me in the corner among protruding springs and crumpled pages of his dissertation. Abruptly he would carry me into the bedroom, drop me onto the bed, undress me, and attempt one of four positions. George had to be reminded of certain parts of the body which he inadvertently forgot. He was a perfectly adequate lover—no more and no less. He was clumsy, lacked subtlety, but was competent. Afterward George often fought or had a wild rage. His approach was traditional, somber, and lacking in any creativity whatsoever.

Not so with Alan. Just as Alan rarely ate at the same restaurant twice, he rarely used the same position over again. There were tepid showers with blue lights or red ones, handstands, knee bends, and somersaults. It was theatrical lighting and gymnastics—things he read about in many manuals or heard about or saw in films or in men's magazines. Alan was an acrobat—was not satisfied until we nearly expired from exhaustion and in my case from exhaustion and boredom. I didn't like the rhythm, the constant changing of position or standing on my head. But Alan could be very romantic and make nice promises while in some precarious position.

Sex to Adolphe, my ex-husband, was almost nonexistent except for an occasional burst with no forward or afterward, only a leap from the bed back to his easel.

—

Melita arrived early in the morning carrying a suitcase filled with her purple clothing and a lunchbox—the same one she had in art school—bursting with brushes and oil paints. She wore a purple suit with green beads, purple stockings, and green shoes. Her long earrings had purple triangles brushing her shoulder. She didn't stop to talk or to criticize the subway system. Melita's eyes were wild. She opened the Frigidaire and pulled out the plums, changed into purple jeans, shrieked with delight at the canvases I had prepared, and that was the end of Melita.

Unfortunately, I had to pass her on the way to the bathroom, and as usual the sight of Melita possessing the plum made me even more nervous than I was. I sat in the other room worrying about seeing my ex-husband, brooding over Auriel's death and Alan's confessions while she obliviously painted, going so far as to hum or sing out loud.

Three days passed and there was no word from Adolphe and no end to the painting of plums and several abusive phone calls from Peter demanding to know what Melita was doing. I didn't dare tell him because Melita said that he was not only drunk but threatening suicide if he ever caught her with a plum again.

On the fourth day my ex-husband called to say he had lost track of time and was coming right over with one of his major works. I took some Stelazine, but it only made me feel rigid and caused my knees to jerk up suddenly. It happened that as I was stiffly waiting the phone rang and a voice sobbed, George is missing, do you have him? I recognized Doctor Clufftrain who said that he had noticed episodes of absentmindedness and even symptoms of senility occurring in George but had ignored them. Foolishly very foolishly, he added. Yesterday he had sent George to buy a T.V. dinner and George had never returned. I assured the doctor that I had not heard from George but would report to him the moment that I did. Melita hadn't slept for two days and suddenly collapsed, looking as pale and beautiful as she used to look when she had mononucleosis. I was about to call a doctor when my ex-husband arrived. The first thing I saw was a huge structure with gigantic spools all wound with cotton thread and a traffic light perched on top. Two panting men carried it inside and plugged it in so the light kept changing from red to green and back again. Adolphe did not say hello, only waited for my response. Melita has collapsed, I said as he sat silently just as he used to sit ten years ago. His arms were across his chest and he was shaking with rage.

I left Adolphe and took Melita to the emergency room at Roosevelt Hospital hoping that no one would recognize me from my previous incarceration. For reasons that elude me or are oddly coincidental, The Alien was there, teaching something about urinary tract infections to a group of interns. He suddenly looked happy assuming that I was about to be committed, then tried to hide his disappointment when he realized that the patient was my friend. Has she been taking drugs or sniffing anything unusual? asked a sloppy looking intern with dull eyes and dirty hands. Only plums and oil paints, I said. He knew nothing about it so he left Melita in a little room and conferred with his colleagues—other ignorant interns who leafed through books or asked nurses. Finally he decided to take a blood sample and give her a complete examination. Rombert watched these proceedings with superior amusement. Does she have mononucleosis? I asked hopefully knowing that mononucleosis would keep her away from plums for a while. No, we think she is pregnant, the intern said. How is it possible, Melita, if Peter is impotent? Melita cried and said she didn't know and she looked very pale and beautiful.

We returned to my apartment in Rombert's car. My ex-husband was motionless except for a perpetual tremor, and the traffic light was blinking green and red all over his face. Rombert decided to cook for everyone. The Alien saw the situation as an opportunity to prove his superiority and mastery over everything and he laughed to himself, British style, as he made a sauce from plums. Melita lay down on the studio cot and wept. My ex-husband waited for some comment about his major work.

Things became worse when Doctor Clufftrain arrived, white and hysterical, with hacksaw in hand. He searched everywhere for George. He isn't here, I said, but he didn't believe me and looked under beds, in drawers, and inside small boxes losing all sense of proportion. Rombert invited Doctor Clufftrain for dinner and the good doctor accepted. The apartment was crowded and confused. I took a deep breath. The spool construction is very exciting, I said, knowing that Adolphe liked the word "exciting." He then began to move and talk very rapidly explaining the spatial concepts of each spool. Here the thread is wound tightly to counterbalance the slackness below and this spool juts slightly forward to provide a shift for the eye as it climbs very slowly to the top and is eventually assaulted by the traffic light. He sounded exactly as he had sounded ten years before.

—

Here in my radiant state of grace the memory of that terrible week turns into a jolly event with people performing antics and reciting lines. It becomes a magnificent play, very rich and diverse and funny. At the time it seemed tragic. I am watching it now like watching a film. In this movie, Melita, giggling, gives birth to a plum—a plum that cries and bites her nipples. Doctor Clufftrain turns into a roach scurrying into everything, senselessly, aimlessly, for all eternity. Even Rombert becomes magnificent in his rose-patterned apron, taking over the kitchen with such grace while Adolphe is no more than an interesting robot making spools and explaining light systems. To me, Princess Esmeralda of 72nd Street, it is all a diversion, play, a vacation from my earthshaking duties. I am singing and serving Rombert's healing, plum-sauced ducks to my guests. It becomes magnificent—a miraculous gathering not to be outdone by the Last Supper. It is a happy peasant's dance around a large table, an orgy under traffic lights—everyone twirling naked on spools of thread—a glowing tapestry is born right now as the moon whirls silently in the night, rabid with the dizzying spectacle of cars, golden constellations, blinking light, and shining doves as Auriel and I rise together into a sky as pure and white as new snow.

—

My head has been hit by a flute. It seems that I went to buy the flute player that Kulack of Bagdad had promised me. I cried out and embraced him, tried to lift him and carry him away. He remembered my dance—the belly dance of a Princess—and the others, all with differently shaped black boxes, packed away their instruments so the room broke or pleasantly wilted like flowers, very quietly. My marionette Plink, or the Pied Piper in plaid pants and rubber shoes, led the night dancers of 72nd Street in leaps and twirls then called at my command for Auriel's doves which came from the other plane hearing the flute-jazz prayer. It was a celestial experience with tears and laughter as the marionette played and played until he was transformed by the very sounds he made into a black knight. Sir Lancelot I called him, and he swore to serve me forever. Then came the dance of life in all its glory as I pirouetted endlessly right here in the throne room.

Then he philosophized in whispers and drank a pale nectar, reaching greater heights of sound with each sip until Orpheus woke up the soul of the entire world and changed the night into day with golden sun popping drops of fire on his flute which he put into me. The sun burned in contrast to cool stars and total evolution occurred as he drank, so things came from his mouth stinging, silver-stinging, not meant to hurt but the morning broke over his head and mine and the flute began to tap me. I saw red pouring away onto the floor but felt only the sound, smelled the ambrosia of his breath, and finally fell.

Today I have made an effort to put cold compresses on the swelling with no memory of how it occurred or why unless some spell was on him from the doves or the hot sun shining in the middle of the night. I feel so beautiful having been touched inside and outside by the sounds of my Knight of the Flute and his miracles. No pain, only sweet-stinging radiance in which no one can be destroyed. I hope it never ends, seven being the number of magic and love and of Venus the White Goddess.

—

I sense from afar that I made my plans for good reasons, but I have not been obeying or consulting my notes. However, some of the rules have become implanted in me like a transplanted heart or pacemaker so that quite without thinking I never disturb the peace. I do not forget to wear clothing despite my tendrils and leaves warmed by the sun. But I have not been trying hard enough, and things were out of hand I suspect from the large lumps on my skull and various cuts and bruises made from broken glass or a flute.

Now I must try to gather myself together. It would be unfortunate if letting it all go where it may, like the Holy Bible instructs, in order to bring forth fruit, I would do it in such a manner as to be locked up. Besides I am quite coherent when I make the effort, which is a very difficult effort almost like changing myself from a dove into a pigeon though all be equal in the Eye of God or Flute, of God or Watermelon, of God or Crown and Scepter.

I hereby gather myself together and focus upon the week when Melita lay pregnant, mysteriously pregnant on the cot and Rombert appointed himself saucemaker. It is tedious as you may imagine to come down from great spiritual heights to talk about these mundane events.

—

By the fourth day Doctor Clufftrain had gone completely berserk, insisted upon looking inside Melita's plums for George. Except for making snide remarks about Melita's paintings and my own which hung all over the apartment, Adolphe said nothing. Things seemed quietly tense but kept under control until the arrival, quite predictably, of Melita's husband Peter who was drunk. He broke out in hives from the odor of rotting plums. Then he tried to jump out of the window and end it all, but the good doctor, despite his preoccupation, was able to summon some kind of reason and reasoned with Peter. You don't need a pregnant wife like Melita who paints plums. You are a man of great distinction and talent, he said as Peter hung half inside and half outside. Soon he came inside and soon his hives disappeared.

Rombert refused to examine Melita to make sure that her pregnancy was not an error. Rombert is like that. If he wants a urine sample it must be given at once. If you beg him to take your pulse or to see if your nipples indicate pregnancy he will take pleasure in refusing.

Deprived of Auriel, mourning him, and cut off from my empire, I was almost nonexistent. I wondered helplessly what they were all doing in my apartment, particularly my ex-husband who acted as though ten years had not gone by and spoke the same sentences. He always had a nasty temper and was very nasty at the dinner table. Adolphe could not tolerate anyone ignoring his creation, and if anyone could ignore a creation of that magnitude and degree of ugliness, it was Rombert. Even Doctor Clufftrain stared absently at the blinking light on top and had spasms in front of the spools. Melita looked it over when she had recovered from the shock of being pregnant. Interesting, she said, and then ran into the plum room giggling. Melita found the idea of making such a construction hysterically funny. Fortunately, my ex-husband thought she had run away from the sight of his work because of jealousy.

Days passed—I don't know how many—but I saw that Adolphe had begun to stare at The Alien with intense hatred. I hated The Alien also but did not care to murder him. My ex-husband had almost murdered a few people in his life and had perhaps succeeded with some that no one found out about. Doctor Clufftrain held Peter's hand but also whimpered about George, prayed, shook, and hallucinated and kept searching. He was heartbroken. When he had given up hope, George arrived drooling and carrying some empty shoe boxes. Doctor Clufftrain had been right. George's mind had deteriorated rapidly, either from some drug the doctor secretly injected into the T.V. dinners or from selling shoes or from the absence of a beard. He put his head on the knee of the doctor and cried. I want my mama, said George. Rombert gave him leftovers and asked him questions about his bladder and urinary tract since George had obviously wet himself. George cried harder and put his face in the doctor's lap. But the good Doctor Clufftrain continued his search. It took him a long time to realize that George was right there clinging to him like a child.

Rombert tried to add laughter and lightness to our days, but no one laughed at Rombert's British jokes because no one had a British sense of humor. Melita expressed no desire to return to that far-off suburb with Peter. All Melita wanted from this world was to paint plums. Adolphe was reaching an acute stage of fury. He began to malfunction and bit Rombert's finger. Rombert, The Alien, was in pain and frightened of rabies. He ran downstairs and reappeared with antibiotics and other chemicals which he administered to himself. By coincidence Alan called and heard the commotion and didn't want to be left out. I no longer cared who arrived. It was all too much, but deserting company is something I would never do.

When Alan arrived, Adolphe was crawling around biting everyone here and there, Melita was painting, and George was walking about drooling and muttering things that made no sense. Doctor Clufftrain was having a spasm and Peter was getting the idea of testing his potency with me or with someone else on 72nd Street. Alan began to express his grief at not being creative, but suddenly he stopped talking and fell in love with Adolphe's construction, which was a relief because my ex-husband stopped biting everyone and began a long recitation to Alan about the spatial relationships of the spools. Rombert having discovered that Melita did not live on West 72nd Street but in a place where there is grass and trees tried to befriend her and agreed to confirm her pregnancy. They were locked in the room together for a long time. Peter was listening to Doctor Clufftrain's story about how he had helped George to find his true identity and George was eating everything in sight. I could tell that Peter wanted to find his true identity also, despite the risks. Occasionally I looked at George wondering how he had ever been handsome and how he had taught a class in the Communist Manifesto and the Russian Revolution at Columbia University. I sang a nursery rhyme and this made George happy. He gurgled and smiled while chewing on a piece of duck.

—

Strange journeys. With or without a touch of radiance I make many trips up and down my kingdom. I see when my people change. It is my job to look after everyone—to see how they are progressing.

Some are stuck to these streets forever like Horatio who interviews everyone with his toy microphone. He complains to me. No one will believe me, but I am made of the moon and I invented glass, the glass of windows, the glass on light bulbs, and glass doors. They don't want to give me credit for anything, he sighs. He would like to become a legitimate interviewer for one of the television networks. I commiserate, urge him to keep trying, tell him not to mind what anyone says. Horatio is twenty-five years old and lives in the Bronx with his mother and father. But this is his street and the Princess acknowledges him. As yet Horatio has not found a woman who is also made of the moon and sometimes this depresses him.

After chatting with Horatio I usually enter the game club and check up to see that the addicts of games are in their usual positions. In reality they are not my subjects. They come from all over—from other counties even—to this gloomy room which is open twenty-four hours a day. Sexless, homeless men, they play out their lives. Really they are grown-up children. Between Radiance 4 and 5 or 3 and 4, I became involved with Leo, a gaunt-faced game addict with a vacant look in his eyes, which I mistook for profundity. In pursuit of Leo, I involved myself in backgammon and struggled until I was an expert challenged by the best. Leo was the very best, and Leo was in the game club every day and every night. Sometimes he would pace up and down and eat a huge meal in the Oedipus luncheonette. He liked to play backgammon with me, liked to teach me more than I knew, and on evenings when the world was empty or full of pain Leo was there. Like Horatio he is a permanent person on West 72nd Street though not a resident.

I finally got Leo up to my apartment. He was childlike at first and pulled his hand away when I held it. But I taught him in the spirit of teaching someone a new game—very slowly and very carefully. He learned it well, but his vacant eyes were perplexed and he expressed no desire to take it up again with me or with anyone else. I guess he prefers chess or backgammon.

The important thing is that the game club be kept in business.

Where would Leo go if it were to suddenly disappear or close down? Where would those other addicts go? They are addicted to this particular street as they are to this particular game club.

Further down from my chess or game club is Rudolpho the genius of hair who failed with all his brilliance and effort to make of my wild hair something shiny, silky, and long. The treatments were endless. He mixed chemicals, feverishly experimented with delicate instruments that measured the depth of the hair in the scalp, its tensile strength, elasticity, acidity, breakage, and protein deficiency. He worked on the outer and inner hair shaft right to the medulla. He tried to strengthen the very molecular structure of each hair. Rudolpho was aglow. My hair was the eternal challenge—the kind of hair that just missed being beautiful, was not irrevocably harmed but needed doctoring, more PH factor, more protein chains. He, Rudolpho, was an M.D. of hair.

This occurred during the beginning of one of my radiances. How could it have gone on otherwise? I was thrilled and he was thrilled as he watched me on my journeys up and down the street, watched my hair change. He became angry if it regressed and turned back into itself. He kept trying. Sometimes I walked out of Rudolpho's Clinique with my hair shining and silky and longer than it is, and I looked like someone else. Tall blonde men followed me complimenting my hair and I didn't know who I was—no longer looked like Princess Esmeralda. Rudolpho became annoyed if the rain or sex or other conditions altered what he had done. He came up to visit quite often bringing the right hair dryers and shampoos and newly invented conditioners. He himself messed up my hair and then put it back and fixed it and taught me what to do to maintain my beautiful hair.

When the radiance came full blown and I was taken away without the implements and chemicals, my hair reverted. Afterward I tried to avoid Rudolpho. I was ashamed to have him see my hair and couldn't endure any more treatments.

Rudolpho is now called "The Wizard of Long Dark Hair," and

people come all the way from the Eastside or across the ocean to have him rejuvenate their hair shafts.

—

I notice, sadly, a recession of Radiance 7, and I can now tell of my ordinary duties and of my life on West 72nd Street without any problems or over-excitement. About being Princess—it isn't that I have ever told Horatio or Leo or Rudolpho or anyone else my title. They sense it somehow. Socrates, the Greek manager of the Oedipus luncheonette, treats me with a mixture of awe and desire. I come close on occasion, say a few words, listen to his particular story, and then I withdraw. It is the same way with all the store managers, bartenders, and many of the residents. There is a trick of appearing not to see and yet seeing everything clearly and precisely. My awareness, although extreme, is never suspected. I know who is pushing drugs in my apartment building, and I know who their customers are. The same is true of those who sell and buy on street corners. I am also aware when someone crosses over from heavy drinking to alcoholism although I cannot be noticed counting his drinks. When someone gains ten pounds, I am the first to notice. It is simply my duty.

It is lonely when the cold comes to 72nd Street, and suddenly there is silence in the apartment and no one to talk to. Then it is more difficult to survey my kingdom. Also those terrible moments—days, weeks, months of detachment, terror, and trembling—things I forget during the heights of my radiance like those long gashes of time between people like Auriel, Alan, or even Rombert. Energy decreases, the live part of me fades or diminishes. Now the radiance has gone out, sizzling like a dead light bulb. Too clearly I see the debris of Radiance 7 like the garbage remaining after any fête or spectacular event. For example, I notice two rotting soggy watermelons smelling sickly sweet. They are invaded by roaches who rush inside and then out and over the crushed tinfoil crown lying nearby. They make a tapping sound on the silver. My bed is ripped apart. The mattress is half off and a rusty spring protrudes. The sheets are stained with thick brownish blood. There is no beauty here—everything is chaotic, displaced, old, worn, and tired. I am. I feel like one of those cheap, sequinned scarves that lie sadly on the floor. Everything has been disturbed and mutilated. It is wrong. The end should be more gradual—not like suddenly hitting the bottom of a pit.

Shouldn't I be happy, though, having passed through Radiance 7 without incarceration, without drugs, without being accosted by the police? Perhaps it is not really over, and if I continue sitting here something will re-trigger its peculiar chemistry and it will return. I hope so. Oh please! It is much too dark. I have no idea how long Radiance 7 has lasted. Why am I covered with bruises as though I have been beaten and raped? My head aches. Where are you my radiance? I cannot bear the stench in this room.

—

It didn't bother me so much that everyone congregated in my apartment that week sometime before my radiance began. It was being deprived of my true identity and having my memories exhumed by all those reappearances that disturbed me. I am certain that George's condition was induced by drugs administered by Doctor Clufftrain. And right there the sacred marriage of Peter and Melita was crushed by the plum conflict and by the intervention of the doctor. The good doctor disappeared. George entered a hospital for neurological observation and Peter—influenced by the words of Doctor Clufftrain—decided to leave Melita and search for his true identity as a man. I believe that Rombert, The Alien, took Melita far away with promises of plum trees and exhibitions. Everything happened slowly and simply as though a pattern had been there all along. For a few days Alan and Adolphe remained, finding much to talk about. Adolphe was flattered by Alan's admiration of his spools and Alan was flattered at being taken seriously by a creative man. I wanted them to leave—all of them. I had wanted them to leave from the beginning. Adolphe finally left silently one morning not even saying good-bye. Alan made another effort to express his feelings for me but I asked him to go. I was left alone with the hideous spool creation until Adolphe sent some men to remove it.

But why had it all happened here—all those changes with myself becoming more and more invisible until I barely existed? I worried about George's condition and feared for Peter and also for Melita who was entrusting her life to The Alien.

I was lonely with the sudden silence and could only dream of my Auriel and his bleeding doves.

—

Radiance has receded further and further, irrevocably I fear, as pieces of stone fall from the sky or from buildings, grazing my fingers as they crack the pavement. There is a sharp chill everywhere and I shudder and walk with difficulty. My legs shake when I walk and my mouth is dry. Is it possible that they will take my kingdom away? I can only walk a few feet and the daylight hurts my eyes. My ribs stick out because I have hardly eaten during radiance.

—

I wash my face carefully, put cold water on the bruises made by falling, made by men I've let embrace me in elevators. Strangers have taken their clothes off here. I let them do whatever they . . . I hide things like belts, socks, engraved handkerchiefs, and combs. Men have left things: coins, train tokens, mailbox keys. It makes me feel ashamed to think of it, to see bluish bruises on my face. I remember some things. Someone threw ice in my face. A silver flute was hitting my head and I didn't feel it. Now I feel the painful throbbing, fill a towel with ice cubes, and place it over the bump on my head. Who will I be when the pain is gone? It burns. Something was shoved inside me. I am no longer radiant. I stand before the bathroom mirror staring into my own eyes. They look dead and there is a yellowish cast to my skin. It is difficult to remember. I see images and try to keep them. Why did the flute player hurt me?

The telephone rings, taking away the vague pictures.

"What do you want? Why are you calling?" I shout, hearing George's voice.

"I just wanted to talk to you, to explain ... you don't have to shout at me. I'm out of the hospital. Did you realize that Doctor Clufftrain was crazy?"

"Of course he's crazy. I knew that."

He is silent, breathing. I can imagine his long red beard and his Persian hat and Persian boots.

"You sound annoyed and preoccupied. Have I done something wrong?"

"No. The phone startled me, that's all. I'm in the middle of ... I can't explain just now."

What right do you have to call me, to intrude, aren't things bad enough, the wreckage, crumbling buildings, stores boarded up without warning

"I want you to come back and live with me ... it's a lot to ask, and I can imagine what you thought seeing me incoherent and regressed ... on the other hand I have so much to give now ... of course I'm completely recovered and may teach at the university in the spring semester. I'm counting on your loyalty."

"I'm glad you are better and there's really nothing to be ashamed of. Just keep well."

You cannot ever torture me again, why should I live with you, you have some nerve after turning me away, what for, you didn't love me, you didn't let me talk or laugh or sing, I did whatever you wanted me to, choked on my silence even, trying so hard to please you

"Do you remember my dissertation? A good academic publisher is interested in it. Think what that will mean for my future ... it will secure my reputation as an historian. You didn't answer my question about living together again?"

"No. I mean I couldn't ever. I'm glad about your dissertation… it should be published… I would be too frightened. You may not realize it but you frightened me with your tearing rags and breaking your bones and conspiring against me."

"Conspiring against you? That's your overactive imagination. Your fear is nonsensical. You know I would never hurt you. I've faced up to my deficiencies. It would be different now… I am no longer as rigid. My expectations of women are more realistic."

"Yes, you might be different… I don't want to, can't you see that. I can't even think about the future… I really have to go now. I'm not feeling well. I have a lump on my head from a fall and it hurts, so I'm lying here with ice cubes on my head… the apartment is a mess… I… what I mean is I don't want to be pressured anymore. I really have to go, George."

"I never meant to pressure you… do you still have that delusion about being a princess?"

"I don't know what you mean. I really don't. I have no delusions. If I ever said that I was joking… that's the trouble, you have no sense of humor."

What business is it of yours, didn't you always barge in at the wrong time terrifying me with the sound of your key, I hate that metallic sound, will you scream at me tonight, push me into the corner or make love to me or make me listen to you read your insipid… what would you know about me

"You know, Ellen, you ought to have regular sessions with a good analyst. I cannot tell you what it means. He'll get at the root of your delusion. You know you have to take responsibility for your own mental health."

"Look, I don't believe in it… not for me… I'm glad your therapist is helping you. Besides I'm perfectly well, I'm just tired and I have to…"

"You just think all psychiatrists are like Doctor Clufftrain. But even he is being helped now... he had a psychotic break. It was building up for years and years. In any event his wife finally left him... but what are your plans, Ellen... everyone must have plans."

"I don't. But I will... I have to work out my life alone... My head hurts so I'm having trouble with this conversation."

"Aren't you even painting? One of these days I'll drop in and we can talk face to face. I'll help you get back on your feet. Then maybe you'll realize that I'm not so bad and that I deserve another chance."

"Please, George, don't barge in on me. I can't stand that. I don't know about painting. It didn't work out. I can't talk anymore. Maybe we can meet and talk some time... I don't know."

"What about today? I'm not far away you know, and it's best to face things to come to terms with reality as it is. I can be right over."

"Not today. I have things to clean up. I am tired."

"It sounds like you're trying to get rid of me. I'm very hurt and disappointed, Ellen, but good-bye."

God, it scares me to have you call, to hear your voice, I would never know who you would change into, your face, the memory of it, frightens me, I don't want to see it again

The light is gone. I feel a weight pressing upon me and it is still difficult to walk. I can barely remember what it felt like to skip down 72nd Street. But I can remember enough to miss the rainbow colors and the immaculate doves. It has ended too soon. Wasn't I spinning with joy just a few days ago? Auriel, if you could only take those bandages off the sky so I could see the stars. Help me come out of this tunnel where everything is damp and cold. Then I could see the moon making the sky light up so even an ordinary tree looks magical. Then I could find my way home through these choking woods. Auriel, is it too late for your illusions? Can't you make me turn into a butterfly? I would fly toward the sun and warm myself. Is it too late for Esmeralda to dance bare-breasted near the yachts. I loved the sound of castanets. Light the windows with gigantic candles. Help me, Auriel. Give me back the magic. Don't let me disappear.

—

The bruises are fading. Even the bump on my head is smaller. It still astonishes me to discover the remains of welts from belt buckles, scratches from nails, and even deep teethmarks. Could it be that I asked, or simply that I never protested, was someone else, while they attacked me? I was radiant then. Even so, some things should never have happened. At least my body should have been treated with respect. I feel empty. It is lonely like after a death or when someone closes the door and disappears forever. Why must they go? They did come for him because he was incoherent and threatening to slash things other than the traffic light paintings. He made movements as though he were slashing at something with a knife. Sometimes he looked at me without recognition and made those movements. Adolphe had not made such movements before except when he was painting. He would stand way back from the canvas and jump forward suddenly, jab at the linen with some pinkish color at the tip of the brush. That was different.

I found the phone number but Adolphe dialed. He even knew who he was calling and that the ambulance was coming. They didn't want me to take any chances with Adolphe in a taxicab. He said he wanted to go. And it was a relief when he was gone with his shivering and teeth chattering and cutting imaginary things or people to shreds. There was a silence afterward. I felt his absence. I stared over and over again at the door through which he had disappeared, proving that I was totally separate and alone. It had happened before. He was my husband and should not have gone away then or on prior occasions when he slammed the door suddenly. I never knew where he was going or if he was ever coming back. He didn't say. It was a way he had of doing things after we were married. It was Adolphe's way of saying something. Not that our time together was pleasant. Even sex didn't interest Adolphe except on a few isolated occasions. Still there was a dreary echo everywhere when he left.

There was a heaviness on my chest like now. I felt like part of me had gone. It was like an arm or a leg being amputated. It was like a death.

Was there something I did to make him leave? I don't mean when he left in the ambulance but later after he came out of the mental hospital in Chicago. That's where they transferred him after he was observed on the psychiatric ward in Philadelphia. I followed, of course. No matter what has happened, it has never been *my* idea to separate from anyone. But I never loved him—not at the beginning not ever. Nor did he love me for that matter. He punished me by his silences. He didn't speak to me or even look at me for days after I admitted disliking the cubists.

"Your husband is what we call, if there are names, a paranoid schizophrenic meaning that he projects his own hostility and deepest fears onto others. He deeply fears his homosexual impulses. He claims you accused him of being homosexual and that you constantly say that he is impotent," the psychiatrist at the mental hospital said.

"Never, although I have complained of his lack of warmth."

"Adolphe told me that you call him names in your sleep and that sometimes when he touches you you turn away, seem almost not to be there at all."

"I don't think so. I don't really know."

Did I do that? Did I turn my back in some subtle way that I never even noticed myself? It is difficult to be sure. It is not hard to remember what others have done, but to notice small actions—movements of my own that are almost indecipherable—it *is* possible that I did turn away somehow despite my outstretched arms. It seems to me that I was gentle and caring and that I did everything he wanted me to do and that I demanded nothing. I even tried to like the cubists. I tried to like his oil painting of a traffic light. The pinks he used were sickening. Often I didn't like him at all. I can remember that. Why then was it as dark as terminated Radiance 7 when he left me for good? He said, "I can't love you or anybody. I'm better off alone." When a husband leaves like that it is the end of everything. Even though Adolphe and I never loved each other.

—

If it were quiet, I might be able to concentrate on getting the fragments of my life together. But there are noises inside my head from all those departures. Although the bumps and sores are fading, my skin burns and stings. Most of the time I rest on my unmade bed. Why must the phone ring? I am startled, nearly jump to the ceiling whenever it does. I don't want to speak to anyone for a long time. Yet I feel so alone.

"I am delighted to hear you sounding so well, so in control of your emotions," Rombert says.

> *You phony you were always happier when you thought I was crazy, who needs you to call you cold bastard*

"Yes, I'm trying to work things through, I..."

"What I really called to tell you is... well, guess, it's good news... can you guess what my good news is? Come on, try... you always had a certain uncanny way of perceiving even though it was a bit convoluted."

> *Leave me alone, Rombert, you and your pee-colored roses and your pompous house where all those trees and grass are as smothering as you, you fat slob, who cares about your good news, that dreary, high-pitched birdsinging hurt my ears*

"I can't guess, really I can't... my mind is on other things. I haven't even the vaguest idea of what it could be. I'm so busy with my..."

"Oh, I'll just tell you since you won't be a sport... I have finally found the woman I have been looking for since the unfortunate loss of my first wife. I'll give you a hint. She is someone you know... a woman of quality, taste, and breeding, and although she is an artist she is not an hysteric and is without any tendency to morbid introspection. As a physician I think that last statement can be taken as diagnostic fact. I even suspect that your Freud would bore her to death as he does me."

You bore me to death, I can just see you walking back and forth on that stale lawn, littered with leaves and dead insects and brown flower petals, what in the world was I doing in that air-conditioned bedroom where you turned me over like a duck in a frying pan

"I've guessed it... you're going to marry Melita. That's nice. Now she can paint her plums. What did you do with Peter?"

"The divorce papers are filed, and he agreed to everything. Then he went to some other country to explore himself, I believe. She's glad to be rid of him after all his carrying on, impotence, and typically American lack of style. In England, where we have never accepted Freud, the character development is simpler, and, of course, our educational system is superior... we don't have so many breakdowns and when we do they are treated with drugs... none of this silly slow psychoanalytic nonsense... we pull ourselves up by our socks. I'm in the process of selling my house as we both prefer Melita's... and it is so close that there will be absolutely no change in my hospital routine."

"Give her my congra..."

"I've got to run... it was so pleasant chatting with you."

What right do you have to marry Melita after torturing me in all those gigantic restaurants and telling me my hair was falling out, who gave you the right to call me shorty, I never said you could, how dare you insult my apartment and my neighborhood and whatever gave you the right to ignore my paintings and to examine Melita in the bedroom, you fat ridiculous

Help me, Auriel. Don't let me lie on this filthy floor in the darkness. Numbness alternates with rage. Don't let this rage paralyze me. I don't want to be alone anymore. Come quickly—before it is too late, before the light goes out forever. Help me wake up. This must be an endless dream of death. Even the fruits taste like ash. There are no textures—only a flat sour smell everywhere. Turn my fear into mist. Make golden flowers appear. Remove this desolation. I want everything to glow softly with blurred outlines. I want people to mean what they say. Please, Auriel. Bring your doves and wigs and silver masks. Love me. I don't even care if it's only an imitation—as long as I don't know—as long as I can't tell. Princess Esmeralda is losing her way—make her live!

What am I doing in Hector's Cuban Restaurant with you, George, how did you manage to persuade me, it would always be like this, my head hurts, it is too soon, it will always be too soon to see you, I find it hard to concentrate, can barely hear what you are saying, your voice closes my ears

"What you are refusing to understand is that it is unfair to judge me by those years... you were not living with me at all, not the real me. Are you listening to me, Ellen? Don't think I don't notice when your eyes dart away... oh, I'm sorry for saying that. God, I've been through so much. Just think of it, Ellen, I had regressed to the level of an infant. Can you ever forgive me? I pray for your forgiveness. You must help me to forget."

"George, you wouldn't even let me sing or speak..."

"Oh God I want to forget all that, it wasn't real. It was all that pressure... the dissertation... broken marriages... You wouldn't hold that against me. I feel that it is only fair that I be given another chance and not be judged by the past. You owe me that... are you following my sequence of thought? Oh, Ellen, don't look so angry. I didn't mean to imply... but I remember your difficulty in following a logical train of thought, some muddy way you had of forming ideas. I don't mean to criticize. I am humble before you."

When I see you with your red beard spread over your chest carefully wiping tears you can make appear at will, I want to scream, I can feel your cossack boots and heels squashing my belly, taste the metallic sound of your key, hear the thunder of huge doors closing and opening, your exits and entrances were always terrifying and often unfamiliar

"George, stop crying and eat your dessert. Lift your head up from the table, the waiter is coming over. You don't have to cry to convince me of your sincerity... but you have to try to understand my feelings... I can't ever love you again... never."

"I see I've made an ass of myself... what a fool I am... all this time I thought you had a forgiving heart, that your love was of a pure caliber... there I was thinking of you all this time and you simply dismissed the beauty of our sharing, our exquisite moments..."

"I disappeared in all that silence and I couldn't find myself anymore... I..."

"Don't talk your metaphysical gibberish to me... you know very well I could never tolerate it. I like the sparse beauty of pure concise thought and rhetoric... I should have known, realized. You've found someone else. No woman can be faithful to one man. You'll all take flattery and caresses from any man. I know how you are. Who is he? Does he have a bigger cock than I? Does he fuck better?"

"Stop it, George. I don't have to listen to you. No, I really don't have to. If you don't stop screaming, I'll walk out and..."

You're only a ghost gulping your coffee and blowing your nose, why am I sitting in this darkness with you, you make me so heavy and tired my head hurts, it is difficult to breathe

"You are perfectly right. I'm sorry. Please forgive me for losing my temper. I'm not perfect you know. All I wanted was to take you here. I remembered that you liked Cuban food. Certainly I don't like it. I wanted to take you to dinner. Is that bad? Is that reason for your hostile disdain? I think I am entitled to see you, considering all the things we've shared."

"I don't want to see anyone right now. There is a weight hanging over me. I need time to work things out."

"Excuses, Ellen . . . just excuses."

"If you could understand about the radiance . . ."

"God dammit. Don't use that crappy act you put on as an excuse. That act allows you total license. It doesn't come out of the air you know. You don't fool me. But I've been a big enough man to forgive you. I don't blame you anymore, even for your disgusting behavior with those men. You must make up your mind that you are ordinary. You are not a princess entitled to do anything you want to."

"That's none of your business. That's what I get for mentioning it to you."

"All I want is for you to be sensible."

"I don't need your advice . . . I'm very tired from . . . I don't know. I haven't slept much in the past few weeks."

"Oh I understand. You've been sleeping around again. You don't have to sit there and cringe. I'm not going to hit you. Who needs you, you look like a walking skeleton. You look like someone's been slapping you around. You can't say that I ever did that to you."

You look so ridiculous standing up with your wallet in one hand stroking your beard with the other, the orange jacket I used to love is stained and falling apart, you look comical, like a copperbearded clown, I am bored by your self-righteousness, it's pathetic how your red beard is full of bread crumbs, you look like a tree for birds

"Wasn't I a good lover at least? Didn't I always make sure you were satisfied?"

"Yes, you were a wonderful and generous lover."

Always very generous picking me up suddenly when you were ready, when you wanted to, even in the middle of an argument or a hostile silence you might be overcome with lust and later on the low bed you did the least you could, that you thought was enough, it never was enough, and you went into a rage, I always feared that your enormous weight would smother me someday

"It's not that easy to find a man who likes to give a woman pleasure. You'll realize that we had something precious and that no man is perfect. Things cannot always be logical or make perfect sense... that is what my therapist says. I am trying."

We leave Hector's Cuban Restaurant and go in opposite directions. That's true, George. Things have never made sense to me either.

—

Radiance 7, please come back and light my way. I never needed you so desperately. Past and present are boarded up with iron nails and crisscrossed slats cover the sky. I can't see the stars. Even your own littered traces are vanishing. I pick up the last of the cue cards. Incomprehensible nonsense. MONEY IS THE MEANS OF BARTER. DON'T SLEEP WITH STRANGE MEN. I thought they were all gone. I could have sworn I'd already snipped those ropes to pieces. Imagine going from typewriter to bathroom like that. There is no end to this debris. I must get it all cleared away. What an explosion was going on inside me. Then it went dark. But I knew from the beginning that this time would be different—even that it might be the last. It may be possible to take a few beginning steps now. Not with this brick wall surrounding me on all sides. Even so.

"Hello, Alan. Oh, not so good. I can't explain it now but if we could simply take a walk—just that. In fifteen minutes."

Alan, with your styled beard, scarab pinky ring, and baroque acrobatic sex, I knew how to get your attention when you were eating pie at the lunch counter, I always have, there is that downstairs bell, I don't like having to ring back and all that waiting pacing back and forth

"Come in, Alan. Oh, thank you, I like orange carnations. Orange is one of my favorite colors."

"Do you really like orange? I wasn't sure. Sometimes I'm not sure what pleases you. I'm glad you finally let me see you ... I was worried."

"There was nothing to worry about. I really like these orange flowers. Sit down. What are you staring at? I know I have some marks on my face ... they're going away. I am well aware of them, and if you want to know exactly where they come from I'll tell you."

Stupid, judgmental Alan, what gives you the right to wonder about my bruises, at least I have something to show for being alive, which is more than you have, disgusting pinky ring

"Calm down, Ellen, I'm not going to criticize you ... I hardly noticed those marks ... I was looking at you because you look like you've lost too much weight, and because I like to look at you. I didn't come here to make you unhappy. You know I've changed in many ways. You know people do change ... at least if they really want to ... even conventional lawyers. Besides I wouldn't be interested in you if you were like everyone else."

"But you'd feel more comfortable. I just can't understand why you're putting yourself through this. Why be defensive about being conventional, materialistic, and a lawyer? There's nothing wrong with it. And why bother with me? Is it some kind of masochism? As you can see everything is all wrong. At least in my life. I'm not even sure what I'm going to do next. What attracts you to me? Why do you keep calling? What do you want? I really don't understand what you want."

"I can't tell you because I don't know myself. Sometimes I think

I'm in love with you. Sometimes I think I am just fascinated because you've experienced things I never have. I think you need me. That's very appealing."

"What things? I don't need you or anyone. I can find my own way."

"No one can. I used to think I could but... Please stop pacing up and down and come here."

You seem so far away like a miniature man with your arms extended, your knees bent, and that scarab ring on your pinky, you don't seem real sitting so far away but I can come toward you like this turning myself into something automatic, only sexual, I am fully aware of myself moving automatically into your arms, something of myself has been left behind, trampled, it could be anyone's arms I know that, who cares, temporary fusion helps the pain, ease the pain for me, Alan, even for a while

"You feel good."

"So do you."

Means absolutely nothing, same words, hold me close and touch me gently and carefully, uhmm, it feels like love, it does

"You see, everything is all right."

"Wonderful."

Accompaniment of penis rising, always a biological phenomenon, no more, not to invent anything, not love, who can love in this world, not me, what about you, Alan, trying to, you can imitate it also, I know better, can imitate it with more conviction, pretend so I almost believe it, I can't either

"Your skin is so smooth, so cool and smooth. I know you don't believe I care about you but I do. If you will only give me a chance to show you I think I could make you very..."

"I believe you, Alan."

Who cares, don't all women have smooth skin, everyone wants a chance to prove something, why shouldn't I believe you now when the feelings are so pleasant, they obliterate all reality, waves of pleasure right up to my head, what are you doing now, why did you have to turn me upside down, my head is brushing the

"Why do you have to do this, Alan? Why do you have to turn me upside down . . . you always drive me crazy with these acrobatics. Why don't you just join the circus? Practice with someone else. . . . I don't like being upside down. Did you ever think of that? You never ask me what I like. I don't think you give a damn who you're doing your gymnastics with. Haven't you heard of simply lying down or of trying to please a woman, of being aware of what she likes?"

"Stop screaming, you terrify me sometimes," he says as his penis softens and falls out. "I thought you liked changing positions."

His voice sounds hurt and his now tiny penis hangs pathetically limp.

"Well, not every second. I hate it. I hate gymnastics. Are we performing for a live audience?"

"You know, Ellen, I never realized what a castrating bitch you are. I don't give a damn about your creativity or originality. I'm getting the hell out of here."

I watch him buttoning his shirt and begin to feel cold. My heart pounds and I am suddenly in a panic.

"Please, please don't go. Please. I want you to stay. I never want anyone to go. No one ever stays . . . all I do is open my mouth once and you run. Can't I say anything? First you invade my privacy and then you run out. Is that fair? You could at least stay until I feel better. Please."

"Stop clutching at me. Get out of the way. I don't think you're worth it. You're a very frightening woman. You think you know everything, you place yourself above me, catch every rotten thing that crosses my mind. Nothing is good enough for you. Nothing in this world. You make me feel so insufficient, so inadequate that it's scary."

"So run away. Everyone always does. You're scary too, turning lovemaking into a martial display complete with fireworks and cheering crowds. Besides, I said I only wanted to take a walk. It's your own fault for not listening. You never listen to me."

The door slams and I stand with my head against it. I would like to bang my head until I can't think or feel this hurt. I would rather be dead or numb. I want Alan to come back. No one ever does. It is so silent after angry words just when I need someone.

At last I cry. I haven't cried in many years.

—

I walk along the street. My street is 72nd Street. Not that it ends there. It is only the center of a radiating star whose points could lead anywhere.

—

Melita is making a large salad in a wooden bowl. Her eyes look outside where it is green. Green is everywhere. In the pool Rombert is floating like a gigantic sea mammal.

"I can paint again," she says smiling, looking at me and then back at the radishes she is slicing. "I hope you don't mind... I mean about my marrying Rombert. I didn't think you really liked him anyhow. Peter went away to find himself... in India. I don't understand what he is doing in India, maybe meditating or something. It's all so complicated. Even in art school I never understood people's complexities or what they wanted from me."

Melita's voice is tired. I observe her flat stomach covered with a purple bathing suit. She has always loved purple. Her eyes have followed mine to her belly.

"I never even wanted a baby. Peter would have been willing at the beginning. I was always that way, not wanting anything more to interfere. I can't help it—it's all too hard. Why does everyone expect more from me? I mean it is so difficult just to wake up each morning and get the clothes organized. You were angry at things I couldn't give lots of times... the same with Peter, even back then when he painted rabbits that he shot. I had to cook them. I couldn't stand touching them and I never ate any. An abortion was the only way for me. It wasn't Peter's baby. It was someone I slept with once, just once when Peter was drunk and threatening to shoot himself with a hunting rifle. It was nothing but he was so kind. I'm not used to that. He's an old professor who used to teach with Peter. He's very happily married. I know I should have taken better care of Peter and that you resent me because I've stayed away from you when you had those... episodes. I can't face anything complicated or unfamiliar. It makes me lose patience and I want to turn away. There are too many things in this world. You can cope with them better than I can."

"No, not really."

I see Rombert standing on the dry grass. The water slides off his body, off his shining, bulging belly. He squeezes the water from his gray beard. It stands out straight from the chlorine. He walks over to a clump of yellow roses.

"He grows roses. Aren't they pretty?" Melita says carefully while slicing the pale green cucumber.

"Yes, I know."

"I always envied the way you could use all those colors and see so many different men and catch on to things quickly. My mind goes so slowly sometimes. All I ever wanted was a quiet life... and to paint."

"And I always envied the way you could simplify things and use only a few colors. He's very critical, Melita, or was it just with me? How can you stand that?"

"I don't mind it. As long as he lets me paint and doesn't keep complaining about his impotence. And I'm just thankful that he doesn't get drunk. I could never stand that. I don't need that much. I never expected as much as you do. Anyhow I'm not such an unusual person and men have never been that attracted to me."

"You don't know how lucky you are that you haven't met so many of them."

"Thank God he likes the house so I didn't have to move. I hate change. I do wish people would admire my paintings. Don't envy me though, because I'm not that happy. No one is ever satisfied with me. He'll probably be unfaithful one of these days. I really wish I could be enough for someone. It even confuses me to cut up all these different vegetables. I would rather make just one thing all the time like a tuna casserole or spaghetti and meatballs but I guess he would get bored."

Rombert, The Alien, the big fat urologist, comes into the kitchen in bare feet and blue trunks. He is smiling, holding the stem of a big brownish-yellow rose.

"What do you think of this?" he asks proudly holding it up for Melita to see. I hear Melita sigh. She pulls herself away from the salad bowl and comes to admire it.

"I like the color," Melita says, and she puts it in a glass of water.

"Ellen likes roses too," he says.

I never did, not for one moment, I never liked hot tea or roses, it was something you assumed without asking

"Yes," I say, not looking at him. The time has passed for telling The Alien that not everyone likes roses, even his urine-tinted ones. I doubt that Melita likes them either. What good would it do to tell him. He goes back outside where it is green. The sun is beginning to burn him.

Melita looks after Rombert as he walks away.

"Do you think you will ever move away from all that noise and garbage? I mean now that things are different. You seem so much better. If you lived nearby we could talk about painting the way we used to. Maybe you wouldn't like it here. There isn't much to do at night."

"I don't know. I've always lived in the city. I can't really imagine it."

"I hope he doesn't keep coming in all day with those damned roses. I like it better during the week when he's at the hospital. He has breakfast there and I don't even have to make his lunch."

I laugh with Melita. It is the way we used to laugh a long time ago before we married Adolphe and Peter.

"But he's really a lot better than Peter, and the sex isn't so bad. At least he's not impotent and thank God he doesn't paint."

"I don't care for men who paint either."

We laugh again.

"What about your paintings?" Melita asks.

"I still have that problem with the colors, but I want to continue and try to solve it. Maybe I can find a way. I know it's not pretty the way the country is but I feel at home there. Anyhow there are many kinds of beauty."

—

To think I see you resurrected in front of Saul the Tailor's. Are you real or is another radiance sweeping over me? No, it is you, Auriel, in plum-colored velvet pants. You haven't even cut your toenails—they come out of your sandals and curve downward toward the ground. My Auriel. My magician. I watch as a white dove appears suddenly and sits on your blonde wig.

I notice some small changes and rearrangements. For example, his cheeks are heavily not lightly rouged and his silver nail polish is no longer on every nail. The alternate nail is colored red—perfect red. On his pale forehead, moist with perspiration, is the familiar silver star outlined in blue. And underneath his velvet jacket—made for illusions—made by Saul the Tailor, is a black satin shirt with gold sequins spelling LIGHT.

In the new illusion the white dove appears from nowhere and sits on his blonde wig cooing. Without a movement of his hand or any apparent prop another dove appears, flaps its wings, and sits on top of the first. The crowd surrounding Auriel is wildly enthusiastic. They applaud and drop many coins and bills into his tapestried bag.

I look at you. No blood is dripping from beneath the dove's white feathers. No scar or sign of strangulation is visible on your white neck.

"I had a lot of trouble sewing in the parts for that trick, and I had to re-seam the whole jacket too," says Saul the Tailor.

No one is listening.

I am watching Auriel's eyes which are half-closed so there is only a faint glistening of gray. Does he see me? I move closer. The birds disappear in a streak of white. Where have they gone? The bird cage on the sidewalk is empty and there are no bulges anywhere—not underneath Auriel's arms or between his legs. His empty hands turned palms up fill with shining stones. And the children say, "Ooh." Amethyst, jade, ruby, many-faceted diamonds seem to come out of the pores in his skin. Pieces of glass throw rainbows into the sky. We clap. He bows from the waist, and the gems vanish like the birds. Auriel's eyes move upward and they touch me, open wide for a second and then close. His lips, painted a silvery pink, break their serene ecstatic smile and twitch slightly. No one notices. They are dropping their last coins and moving quietly away. Some congratulate him and shake his soft palm.

"You are still beautiful," he says as the doves appear from the air and are gently placed inside their cage.

Such gentle hands would never hit me over the head with a flute, Prince Auriel, take me to that land of sensuality where I am princess

"Someone said you were dead . . . had strangled yourself with a rope. I didn't know for certain . . . hoped you would return."

"Mean Marsha made that up. I don't live with her anymore. She wouldn't let me see pretty women and she told everyone I was dead. I was mad at first, screamed and threw things against the wall . . . then I liked it. It seemed like a prophecy . . . that my material self should be dead, should even die violently while my soul became purified . . . part of the white energy that is the entire universe.

I have always wanted to surrender my individual self... it was like a prophecy... so I hid away with her and no one could find me. I did nothing but practice the teachings of Guru Maharaj-goo. I do not think I will shed my material existence during this karma... I discovered that I am even lower than I thought."

I listen. Auriel has forgotten how I, Ellen, despise the teachings of the Guru Maharaj-goo.

Automatically we walk in the direction of The Copper Hatch as we did the day we met. At the table which is surrounded by false glass, Auriel takes off his blonde wig and laughs a child's laugh—very high-pitched.

"I remember when my wigs frightened you."

"Yes. I have been inside a dark tunnel for years and years... I am just trying to come out."

I can tell the truth to Auriel, my prince

"What kind of tunnel—what is in it?"

"It is full of grotesque forms rotting and distorted from the damp darkness—things I was afraid to look at in daylight. I still don't want to see them. I am trying to."

Auriel takes my hand in his soft hand with the nails alternating silver then red.

"You seem to be on a dangerous base plane... almost in hell. It is evil to be there. You could destroy your soul forever in such darkness," he says squeezing my fingers.

"It is better to emerge slowly."

A prince would understand, a prince would cheer and applaud, don't turn away, help me

"You must only go forward because all those forms you see in the tunnel are unreal. They are base illusions. The real world is one... it is white light."

His lips form their serene smile and he looks at me with half-closed eyes.

"I am going forward but very cautiously."

Why don't you say, I love you, why do you look so far away, we can go home and paint our bodies gold

"Where is Princess Esmeralda?" he asks suddenly, sharply.

Will Auriel leave me again

"She is inside me."

I do not know where she is or where to find her

"I don't see her. I can't find her anywhere. I don't think you are Princess Esmeralda."

"She's right here. Don't you see her? Anytime I want to I am the Princess. You are blind . . . you are blinded by white light. I've been waiting for you all this time for so long."

Where is Princess Esmeralda

"You lost her in that hideous place. I can feel things like that because I have a special sensitivity. I can see how the mud came and swallowed her and left only you. I wrote a note saying, I love Princess Esmeralda. Marsha got angry and tore it up. That's when she called you and said I strangled myself. I loved Esmeralda so much. She had a shining beauty . . . something silver."

I am losing you, you look at me with suspicion, even at these tears

"Maybe I'm wrong. Even I go backward sometimes. Sometimes I too am low and blind and lost. Please let me love you. Maybe you are still Princess Esmeralda."

Auriel puts down the bird cage as soon as we are inside. And he takes off his blonde wig. Heavy rouge, lipstick, and the silver star remain.

We lie down. Auriel pulls his paintbox from the bottom of his tapestried bag. Slowly with the smooth sable brush he paints green daisies on my breasts. Then he kisses them. Five orange spiders tickle my thighs. Silver moons shine between my toes. All the flowers start to quiver. He transforms my navel into the purple mouth of a long-breasted Satan. Then he turns me over and slides his tongue down my back. Luxurious circular pinched kisses move on my buttocks and a sweeping line goes up my spine exploding at the nape of the neck. I moan and he rolls away from me and laughs.

"An insane butterfly with an antennae to God," he says.

I roll back against him so my rosebush buttocks touch his thighs. Softheaded his penis electrifies those leaves and petals scattered everywhere. This pleasure is almost pain. The bumblebee darts here and there with a caress, pinch, or lick of the tongue. It flies away. Nothing in the world could be wrong. Each cell blossoms, beating hot sun. Sweet dew is pulled from multiplying fingertips.

"You are beautiful whoever you are," he says surveying my swirling thighs and fast-breathing breasts.

I watch as he puts his fluttering penis inside a transparent balloon—blue-veined moon god inside a big bubble. Singing, he outlines his own nipples with black lines thinly going round. Light-tipped they meet mine with a shock. Time bursts forth giddy and comical as a carnival. The slow Ferris wheel dips into a dusk of glowing cells lit up, slowly brightening with incandescent light. Black net sweeps gently over artificial clouds. From way up here I can look down on moving light-rhythms about to explode. The moon is biting my fingertips in the dark night. Finally the separate colors and defined boundaries of form slip away. All is fused in ecstatic giggling. Never complete, teased endlessly, endlessly resting, changing color or design with infinite spectrum of violet. The silver star bursts, turns to liquid on his forehead as the painted orange spiders kiss the moons between my toes. A silken water veil is spinning over us—joy we create together in time's peculiarly perfumed medium. Isn't this my afternoon and night of the absolute? This prince awakens me—an awakening drawn on through all eternity as long as sleep and short, and as absolute as green—a dark rush of cells squeezed and drenched in this biting flamebath. No atom or any part left out. If death were like this.

But I can hear the flute sounds of my cruel knight. Why do I hear that hell fife? Its sound bruises me.

"Do you know who I am now?" I ask from inside this pleasure net of toes and heads mingled into each other—formless jelly drip of angels.

"You are the Evil One disguised. You are the one who keeps me on this heavy material plane. You are another omnivorous, anonymous sensual female. All of you are one—the original Eve, first wife of Adam . . . Lilith the Evil One." He laughs.

All the rainblown glass cracks on the edge of the world. My skin is coated with scabs which feel no flame. Nothing now. Eternity vanishes.

"I don't mean these things. Something inside me makes me say them."

He notices the quick closing of the pores of my skin—drying up of dew sent out by sweetened cells. Now clogged with poison the molecules can't breathe. I shiver and dry silver flakes fly into the air.

"You are the only one who lets me do anything I want to . . . the only one who likes . . ."

"I'm not interested."

"With the others I sometimes have to beg to draw a little daisy anywhere. I like that. I like when I have to beg to draw a daisy. You let me do everything so it's not as much fun."

"Get the fuck out or I'll kill you," I say quietly.

My prince shudders.

"Don't be so angry. I never said I loved you. I never even called you. You have no right to be so rude to me after all the pleasure and the time I have given."

"Get out or I'll take this cage and kill the doves. I'll drop the whole thing out of the window."

I am running around my apartment with the cage of fluttering doves. Auriel, my false prince, is running after me with his penis dying inside a transparent balloon. His forehead star is just a puddle on his nose.

—

Is beauty always demented? I am running away from my old vision of a prince. These streets are cold and motionless. I don't understand. Even time seems frozen so it takes me so long to go down into the basement ballroom of 72nd Street. I am alone. This time there is no lover named Kulack wearing a jacket of brocade and tossing jewels and coins into the sky. I enter the large room and hear the sound of electric instruments and of a flute. But there are no Arabian princes anywhere. My eyes without the magic veils of Salomé hurt at the sight of him. I am unarmed. Is this Sir Lancelot of the Flute or Plink the Puppet?

He sees me but keeps bouncing puppet-like with his rubber shoes. He wears a wig that comes down over his forehead like orange straw. I am sitting quietly in my long skirt with its rose flowers and my rose-colored tank top. Does he recognize me? My hair is not gleaming with vaseline. No sequinned scarves wind around my waist, and only the thinest line brightens my eyes. I do no gorgeous belly dance, no fluid undulating dance of Salomé. He recognizes me. When the set is over he slowly, so slowly, puts his flute away and walks to my table.

"You're not stoned tonight," he says.

"I wasn't stoned then . . . it's hard to explain."

How can I explain even to myself why I didn't scream or cry when you banged my head with your flute

"Come on baby, you were out of your mind . . . beautiful."

"I don't like to be hurt."

I see your wrinkled face, bald head underneath the orange wig, just an old man in sneakers and plaid pants pretending to be young, such bloodshot eyes, dark rings underneath, inside your eyes you look cold like the shine of a flute, an old man who gets pleasure from giving pain

"I don't like pain."

"The hell you don't." He laughs. He laughs only with his mouth. His eyes are still and ice-cold.

I know you wear a wig, baldy

"You hurt my head, and inside me there was bleeding."

"You asked for it honey. I dig you but I'm tired tonight. I've got to keep cool. Have a drink on me."

"No, thank you."

Baldy with outdated slang trying so hard to be

"Whatever you say. There's no shame in being what you are. Do your thing. It's my thing too. It's the way we can get it on. Right? Come out of the closet baby. Right? Different strokes for different folks. That's what I say. Look do you want me to call you?"

"I don't like to be hurt."

He laughs and goes back to the other musicians who are shoving aside their drinks and stamping out cigarettes. No magic here. Everything is drab and old. I leave the flute-jazz sound which is like thick decaying honey. I climb up to my crumbling street.

I killed my knight of the flute and my prince of white light.

—

It happens that I don't need ropes to tie me to this typewriter. I keep coming back of my own free will. It is because of my sorrow about these deaths, including the deaths of princes. And I have no schedule. I haven't worked since George stopped me from teaching arts and crafts to senior citizens. Some money comes from disability. During Radiance 5 a social worker decided that I was eligible for Medicaid and other assistance. I am sorry to admit even to myself that I have lately been listless about my duties regarding this realm. I can feel no enthusiasm for daily inspections.

It is in this lack of spirit and low sense of commitment that I make my tours. I make them at random. In fact, I hardly care who sneaks in through the opening on the Eastside of the park. The bicycle lanes have stopped worrying me. You see, I am only a shadow of myself. I don't know what to make of it. I am a mystery even in my own eyes. All people are full of secrets.

On another night, for example, that flutist Plink told me about his long marriage to a beautiful woman who sang jazz songs "something like Billie Holiday," if you want to believe him. And that it was one of those rare kinds of marriages that work. Suddenly cancer invaded her pelvis—a little at a time. It was "a slow death." She kept singing even though she was going in and out of the hospital for so long. "It was too long for anyone to bear dying. Dying shouldn't ever take that long." Plink said all these things—that same Plink who hit me over the head and screwed me with his flute during Radiance 7.

"Afterward I changed," he said, "stayed by myself, shot up some, drank. But I couldn't screw." He said "screw."

"Then I met a broad who turned me on to pain. At first I thought it was sick. But I could get it off. I hadn't even thought about it before if you know what I mean. Maybe it was inside me all the time. Who knows what's inside that never sees the light of day? God, it scares me to get old alone like this but, well you know, at least I was happy for a long time. Not many people are. I still shoot up sometimes but not often. I don't want a habit. And then I get it on sometimes with someone who's into my thing like you. Life isn't so bad except when I start remembering what she went through at the end and how she looked. Our daughter married a shrink, lives in Huntington, Long Island. No problems. She's not into music and I'm glad. And I have two granddaughters sweet as sugar. I miss her. Janis was her name… Jan. God how I miss her."

He told me that story one night when I was down there again.

What I don't understand is how someone like that can bang women around. He almost killed me. I see all these things now. I see things differently—from all sides. But I miss the way it was and how I used to feel in my kingdom before Radiance 7.

I got a letter yesterday from my crazy ex-husband Adolphe, the bastard. Never cared about anyone but himself. We got married because everyone else at that art school was doing it:

> Dear Ellen,
>
> Thank you for your hospitality when I was in New York City. Although I never wrote, I did think about you during those ten years subsequent to our unfortunate divorce. I say unfortunate because I think we were good companions in many ways. You were someone I could always discuss my theories of art with. Sometimes I felt, though, that secretly you wished me ill. Perhaps we would still be married if it wasn't for that traffic light painting episode. That someone would steal such a virginal idea from me is something I still find despicable and beneath my contempt. No doctor has ever convinced me that it was a coincidence. How could anyone else have had such an idea? But fortitude has its rewards. I've always been convinced of that. I vowed to work hard and to succeed, and succeed I have, as you yourself have witnessed by the greatness of my work.
>
> My faith and idealism are often misconstrued and misunderstood and resented. My subsequent wives were also jealous of my creativity. I think people place too much emphasis on frivolity and sexual activity. The only solution to my own misfortunes has been discipline and hard work, which does

not, by the way, mean I am a repressed homosexual as you always secretly believed.

A new avant-garde has arisen and I am one of its great innovators. This is not bravado but simple truth. One should either join the new avant-garde and realize that painting is dead, or be buried alive. I am afraid that you don't seem to realize that there is no more painting. *Painting is Past.*

They are out there everywhere waiting for me. I will speak to them. Do you understand me better now? I am a man with a difficult mission. I am paving the way for other artists in my expression of the fourth and fifth dimensions. I use the equations of Planck as a guideline for my spool and traffic light works. Heisenberg is also relevant to the relativity of spool placement and frequency of light flickering.

My Best Regards, Gracious Thanks, and Love,

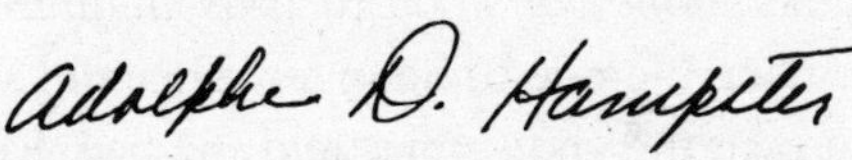

Adolphe D. Hampster, Ph.D.

I am touring my kingdom. It is like taking a long voyage through uncharted land. I have never been here before—at least not this time or in this way. Columbus also set sail with maps he couldn't depend upon. My explorer's costume is a floor-length skirt patterned with a yellow and black abstract design. Hanging from my neck is a huge silver owl with amber eyes.

I am dressed to fulfill a lost title, I think, spying a row of black plastic garbage bags. Days pass and no garbage truck appears. They look like elegant monuments. I walk around them and enter the Oedipus luncheonette on the corner of 72nd Street and Columbus Avenue. (It is here that I met Alan by displaying my breasts.) That was a long time ago.

At one of the tables sits an actor—a black policeman on one of the ABC television soaps. He is staring out the window at the line of full garbage bags. Across the street is a small expensive supermarket. It was there that I once stole grapefruits and toilet paper. I was wearing a transparent nightgown. (It was called the Ruxton then.) Two opera tenors are eating from one plate and passing a music score back and forth. They are chewing rapidly.

The Argentinian pianist sighs and sits down on the stool beside me.

"I have sold my record store."

He taps his fingers on the smooth counter and I recognize Ravel's *Bolero.*

"Are you feeling well?" I ask, remembering that he looked pale the last time I passed him. That was another time (before Radiance 7) in an entirely different kingdom.

"Well, who can feel well without money? I'm bankrupt. In fact the whole economy has collapsed. A dollar is worth nothing and no one wants to spend money on good records anymore. You used to come in. I remember. No one came in anymore so I sold it... that's life I guess. You take the good times and the bad. Right? My wife isn't feeling good either... it aggravates her. God knows I was meant to be a great pianist and I never should have gotten married... oh well, no use crying over spilt milk. You look nice as usual. Are you on one of those crazy diets?"

"No. I'm sorry about your store... and that you won't be here anymore," I say feeling that it is my fault. I avoided him and haven't been inside his store for months.

Is it my fault when someone goes away

"At least summer is over... it was such a hot summer," Socrates, the owner of the Oedipus says.

"So what are you standing here for? Go wait on the customers," he says to a handsome Greek waiter whose eyes are watching the woman passing outside. He says something in Greek and laughs. Socrates looks out of the window and laughs also. The woman waves. She has enormous breasts and wears tight pink pants which sink into the indentation between her thick buttocks.

Thou shalt not covet thy neighbor's wife

The door opens.

"So how are you, Tony? I don't see you around." Socrates extends his hand to a little old man. He is ancient and stooped over like a dwarf.

"The season is over. Men are getting laid off... I don't know... they'll probably let me go... an old man like me. Who knows?"

He sees me sitting there with my owl eyes and smiles. I remember and my heart beats rapidly. I remember someone else, not me, lying in Tony's arms. A tinfoil crown is on his head and watermelon pits are all over the floor.

Bursting red fruit and sweet perspiration everywhere, I want to hide from this memory, it glistens like a red jewel clearly cut, my little King Lear who planted pits inside me on a hot afternoon

"Hello, gorgeous," the dwarf says, touching my cheek with the back of his hand.

Socrates and the three Greek waiters stand watching like marble sculpture. The opera singers are also watching and the soap opera policeman has his gun ready.

"I tried to call you but there was no answer. I even rang the downstairs bell a few times," he says loudly while his rough old hands climb over my face and hair. His fingers squeeze my shoulders like claws.

"Oh, I was sick. I fell on my head and I had a lump and a headache."

How could I have with a tiny old man, a dwarf with greedy eyes, broken teeth, and black fingernails, why, everyone knows, they are all watching

"I'm sorry to hear that you were sick. Do you still love your Tony?" he whispers in my ear.

"Yes... of course," I say, wanting to disappear.

"Don't you think you're a little too young for her?" asks the Argentinian pianist still tapping *Bolero* on the counter.

"Too young, too old, not Tony... Tony does it well, what do you think?"

The Greek waiters laugh. So does Tony. The opera singers begin to shake with laughter. There is too much noise. The black garbage bags appear menacing.

"No, let me pay," Tony says as I hand Socrates a dollar bill and some change.

"No, thank you," I say.

Socrates pushes my hand away. "It's on the house... anytime... for you, sweetheart. Anytime."

They all look at Socrates and smile.

I push the door open and run out tripping over my long yellow skirt. Tony runs after me.

"Don't go so fast, I can't keep up. Would you like a little company? My truck is parked across the street and I have nothing to do... nothing to deliver for the rest of the day. I'm free," Tony shouts laughing and running after me on his tiny legs.

"No, thank you," I call out turning my head and trying to smile.

The soap opera policeman is standing with his hand on his gun watching.

Suddenly Tony gets angry and his little old face turns red. He waves his muscular tattooed arm in the air.

"If I was good enough for you once I'm good enough for you twice. Who do you think you are? Tony will tell you what you are. You're a *tutti-frutti,* a nut."

He looks so furious... an ancient angry dwarf, a spiteful elf.

It wasn't me don't you understand, I'm not responsible for that day, it was a gift of Radiance 7, can't you try to understand

"I'm sorry I can't help it. I don't feel well," I shout.

I see nothing but black garbage bags as I run up the street. They stink up the air with their rotting odor. Tony is shaking his finger at me and cursing with his arms.

"I don't sleep with no sluts. You're a crazy slut. You're a *tutti-frutti.* Who do you think you are, making fun of an old man?"

—

I am here, hiding at my typewriter. Tony is still running after me and the soap opera policeman has his gun ready. There is always a punishment for radiance. I had forgotten. People hate it when you are happy for no reason, or when your personality changes. I used to become a water lily. They like everyone to act the same way forever.

Usually I am incarcerated and treated with chemicals. In fact the most highly esteemed chemotherapists have gathered around me in hospitals. Not this time. The punishment is different.

My heroes of radiant days and nights have come back to haunt me. Tony may murder me for not being radiant forever—for not being able to crown him as dwarf king. Who ever promised you that anything would last forever? Even I know better now. Plink could easily insist upon his right to bang me unconscious every night. They feel certain things to be their rights and destinies. I don't blame them. I wouldn't blame myself if I shot Auriel in his swinging scrotum for not continuing to worship me.

It is the backlash of Radiance 7 flying in my face. Hate and rapture bumping into each other. Even those ordinary sidewalks have gleaming stones mixed in with the cement—they shoot stars into my eyes.

Someone cared enough, had enough faith to carve lion's heads on the edges of brick houses. There are even gargoyles with alligator skin jutting from cornices of 72nd Street buildings. On the other hand, a papaya stand has replaced Orange Julius and Sean O'Reilly's ordinary orangeade counter has become a health food emporium. Not even mundane things are predictable. Everything, I suspect, is two-headed.

Resuming my perilous walk, I stop at the papaya stand. Horatio has followed me down the street past the Japan Art Center where I bought an acid-green straw hat, past Fine and Schapiro's Delicatessen, past the Chinese restaurant where I once deliberately threw a teacup against the wall. It was when Alan's eyes were darting on the breasts of a blonde giantess.

"Are you made of the moon?" Horatio asks, forgetting who I am. "You see, I am looking for a woman who is also made of the moon with an indented navel."

He stares into my face as though we have never met. Each day is brand new for Horatio. He holds his toy microphone in front of my mouth.

"I am sorry but I am not made of the moon."

The papaya stand is crowded.

"I am the inventor of glass—the glass of windows, carlights, panes, storefronts, and telescopes. Won't anyone give me the credit that I deserve?"

Horatio shoves the microphone in front of Leo, the game club addict, whose vacant stare I once mistook for profundity.

"I think you're getting a little mixed up, man. Why don't you cool off with an orange juice?" Leo says.

Leo avoids my eyes. He doesn't want to remember anything about the game I taught him on one of those nights when the world seemed dead.

"I just beat Gus at three games of backgammon," he tells me without looking into my eyes... "I don't see you playing anymore. You were good." He looks away.

"You look like your eyes come from the very center of the moon," Horatio is saying to a young hooker. She is wearing maroon boots and a pair of tiny black satin shorts. Her skin is pale white and her curly hair is dyed light orange.

"Sure, why not," she says without a smile. She doesn't care. She is tearing the frankfurter with her hard teeth, staining the roll purple with her lips. Her blue halter is spotted with mustard.

"Do *you* believe that I invented glass?" Horatio asks looking into her heavily lidded old old eyes.

"Sure, why not," she says without looking at him.

Horatio looks at her long white legs. Her black friend with high tiny pointed breasts showing through a tied midriff marches in. Her straight skinny legs stand on green monster platform shoes.

"Hey, come on, Marie," she says, putting her arm around her friend's slim waist.

Outside the window stands Willie Hoover wearing his big black cowboy hat studded with rubies. It ties underneath his chin. Pearl buttons hold his silver shirt together. He stands high on great silver boots. I count eight silver rings with eyes of tigers, eyes of tomcats. He doesn't turn his head, just stands there so still, hardly breathing. He glitters black and silver. His Cadillac is decorated with painted heads of leopards. And inside the seats are covered with leopard skin.

Marie dabs at the mustard spots on her blue halter. They walk outside and stand on either side of Willie. All three enter the Cadillac and drive away. Horatio looks after them.

"She is made of the moon like I am. I need her," he says sadly.

"I never beat Gus before," Leo tells me.

I stand at the counter drinking papaya juice and watching as Horatio crosses the street. Leo returns to the 24-hour game club to shake Gus's hand.

—

Dutifully I look into Rudolpho's Clinique. Rudolpho sees me and comes out of the shop wearing his white tunic. He runs his hands through his thick graying black hair.

"What have you done with your beautiful hair? I told you that a treatment every four months is essential. If you're not going to do what I tell you, this is the kind of hair you'll be stuck with—thin and curly, dead medulla, weak cortex, too much elasticity, split ends. Look, all the ends are split."

He squeezes a bunch of my hair in his hand and makes a face.

"I told you not to have intercourse without wrapping your hair first. Just wind it around your head with a few clips—all that perspiration is as bad for the hair as chlorine. Ugh! Come on in, honey, I have some new things to show you. Come on. I'll give you a treatment and wrap your hair. No charge. It hurts me to see you looking like this.

"Come, sit here," says Rudolpho, putting a towel around my neck. He pushes close to me with his erection and kisses my ear.

"I'm going to use a new shampoo on your hair. It tames curly hair by giving more weight to the cortex." He squeezes my thigh. I remove his hand, but I let him wash my hair, treat it under ultraviolet light, and wrap it around my head in one smooth sweep.

"I know it's none of my business, but what's going on with you? I've seen you with some strange looking men this summer. You're not on drugs are you? You know drugs will kill your hair and scalp. See, your scalp is tight from tension. No blood circulation. Why don't you let me come up after work say about eight, and I'll give you a scalp massage. You don't need drugs, sweetheart. I can give you what no drug can."

"I'm not on any drugs."

Rudolpho, the hair doctor, has lit the flame torch and is burning off my split ends. I can smell singed hair.

"I saw you a few times with a lot of grease on your hair. You should know better. Just run your fingers through your hair if it looks dull—the sebaceous glands under your skin will give you all the shine you need . . . come on . . . don't push me away, I just want to kiss you. Why not? I see you with plenty of old men, drunks, and addicts. What's wrong with me? If you can screw those characters why can't you be nice to a perfectly normal, healthy, attractive middle-aged man who adores you?"

He puts the large dryer over my head.

"I don't like the word 'screw,'" I yell from beneath the hood. "I haven't been 'screwing' anyone. I just have all kinds of friends—friends of all ages."

"O.K. Don't get excited, but remember it's your friend Rudolpho you are talking to. I see everything that goes on in this crummy neighborhood."

"So do I."

The dryer is lifted off my head and he takes out the clips.

"You know I won a prize at the big hair show at the Coliseum. I would have done your hair and used you as one of my models but you stopped coming in ... maybe you were avoiding me ... anyhow I won the prize for long-hair styling and treatment. First prize—it was in all the papers."

"Congratulations. You really deserved to win."

"Thanks. You know in many ways I'm a very conservative man. I take good care of my wife and kids. Well, now they're almost grown up, but I was always a good father. And I'm not into liquor or drugs—not even grass. In that way I'm very conservative. Of course you know I'm a health nut. But with sex I'm a liberal. However, no matter what goes on with me sexually, and plenty does, I'm always discreet. And I'm not saying this to hurt you or because you've rejected my advances, but every man in this neighborhood knows you're an easy lay. Honey, people have eyes. You can't pick up men in public and drag them up to your apartment in broad daylight without people seeing ... like I saw you one afternoon with a worker who had a safety pin holding his fly together and plaster on his boots ... not to mention a red face from too much boozing. What's the matter with you! I saw you take him upstairs, and I saw him come out a couple of hours or so later. It looks bad, honey, very bad. I thought, she couldn't be in the business ... but then why else would she do it? Do you need money for something, dear ... tell me and I'll lend it to you. You're not a stupid lady."

"I'm not a prostitute if that's what you mean. Besides, it's none of your business. There are things you wouldn't understand."

My lips are quivering and the tears are about to fall. I hold them back but he sees one or two escape.

"Hey, don't cry. I didn't mean to insult you or to sound like a judge. I'm not in a position to judge anyone. I'm really concerned about your welfare. Would you believe that we swing... my wife Ruthie and me? Maybe once a month we do it. We both enjoy it and it's brought us much closer together. I like to see her enjoying herself with another man. It turns me on. Good clean people of course. But no one knows. We don't advertise it."

"I believe in monogamy, in being faithful to one person," I say softly.

"O.K. O.K. Let me comb out your hair. It feels silky now." He smells it.

"Look at the shine. You are going to be gorgeous when you walk out of here. Don't waste it, honey. Don't waste it on any bums... get a guy who has something to give you. Don't sell yourself short... and please wrap it and wear a scarf if you go dancing or if you do anything else that might make it frizz up." He smiles.

I walk outside with my hair long and straight and shining. Is it my hair? It bounces up and down. Is it Rudolpho's? The wind blows through it softly. But I am worried. Who else will I see from Radiance 7? Who else has watched me and misunderstood? How will I convince anyone that I believe in absolute monogamy and that I am opposed to all the things I am accused of? Who are they to pass judgment anyhow? Aren't these my streets?

I wave back to the old shoemaker who has gentle eyes. He was away for a year after massive heart failure. A dead person's heart pumps blood into the veins of his hands. He has never married. I know these things. He waves to me as I pass.

I had no intention of upsetting Tony. Is it my fault that the Argentinian pianist must sell his store and move away? Have I neglected my duties? Was it wrong to visit the flute player again or to threaten Auriel with the demise of his doves? Would it have been better if they had locked me up? Should George be given another chance even though he almost drove me insane? Can a man be expected to keep his eyes in front of him? Is it demanding the impossible? Who will help me with all these questions?

I feel lost these days as though my kingdom has vanished and my title has been confiscated. I have doubts about everything—even about the ten commandments. I doubt my ability to gain respect, admiration, and obedience. But other leaders have lost their kingdoms, have even elected to become ordinary citizens in order to enjoy simpler pleasures. Sometimes I, too, am tempted to give all this up—who needs it anymore? I may abdicate.

MY ABDICATION AND BEGINNING

It isn't easy to give up a title and a way of life; the implications are terrifying. For one thing, the ticking of hours becomes distinct. There is nothing to protect me from the usual aging and death. Eventually I may lose all my teeth and become bald. I am susceptible, now, to hundreds of bodily invasions including cancer, heart attack, and kidney failure. I used to believe that I was somehow beyond ordinary time-connected deformities. In those eternities of radiance I may have already lived for centuries.

It isn't easy. I have, in fact, fallen to earth with a bang. It wasn't deliberate. I have lost the key or the route to radiance. Even royalty eludes me—that way of passing through everyday events—and plain talking is gone. Princess Esmeralda has vanished or stepped aside.

I am only now learning to speak—that is—finding a way of translating myself so that I won't remain invisible. My crown and scepter made me visible before—to others as well as to myself. It all has to be done without cue cards or any other external aid. Even when I cannot think of anything to say or find a situation overwhelming or perplexing, I can no longer turn into a blade of grass or a pearly-scaled fish. That hurts. I am so naked that my hands seem to hang heavily from my wrists. I can feel my bones age. My God, I never noticed how hard my legs work to carry this weight around. Sometimes though, my feet plant themselves into the ground holding my weight like strong roots and I experience a sense of strength. Other times I feel less sure, fear that gravity might fail and plunge me spinning into eternal emptiness.

Someone forgot me—long ago—underneath a table mumbling in a language known only to puppets, princesses, and rocks. My world became a composition of water, light, sunstruck pebbles, bell-like birdcalls. A princess can, of course, turn any passing truck into an ocean wave, a stranger into a prince, debris into jewels. I created that world and I have destroyed it. Sometimes I hurt all over and miss Esmeralda. There is no turning back I am afraid.

—

I didn't see Alan for several months after his penis collapsed and slid out; I thought he had run away from me forever. But, to my surprise he didn't seem to hold it against me and began to call again. He kept on calling. I couldn't understand why. I had criticized his lovemaking and had also clung to him hysterically. No man of my acquaintance has ever forgiven such flaws. Besides I was no longer enchanted. I had stopped parading about 72nd Street with almond-shaped black lines emphasizing my yellowish eyes and I looked less remarkable with Rudolpho's straight hair, tiny earrings, and missing neck pendant. In addition I now wore a brassiere and had stopped wearing some of my more spectacularly color-splashed floor-length skirts.

My interests were gone! I couldn't care less what was happening in the game club or if it closed for that matter. Nor did I concern myself with the volume of clients in Rudolpho's Clinique. My desire to improve the lives of the residents had simply vanished into thin air.

What could Alan possibly want with me now? I hardly remembered how I had held on to his penis upside down with no hands without scraping my head on the floor. Sometimes I was tempted to see him, though, because of being so lonely—bereft of a kingdom, without respect or responsibility except for the one assignment I gave myself. It had to do with color purification for my self-portraits. In fact I found three colors for my head and three different levels of light and dark. I forced myself to use only these. Imagine how hard that was for me, with the light changing constantly and new colors appearing, so that it took all my willpower not to add viridian green, ultramarine blue, violet, crimson, cadmium red, and pale ochre to the tip of the nose. It was a task so difficult—almost as impossible as asking Melita to reinvestigate the colors of a plum. She would die if she were forced to change her color combination or to add even a speck of moss green.

I refused to see him. I did not feel I could keep my wishes quiet anymore even for the sake of yielding to the particular proclivities of his penis—its need to penetrate from angles opposed to gravity. No, Alan, I can't be that accommodating nor do I want to frighten you by shouting out against your mechanical lovemaking. I was tempted though, because my hands hurt from being so heavy and untouched. He might at least hold my hand if he felt up to it.

Alan often sent me orange carnations and asked me out to dinner. But I was not ready to dine out formally and be subjected to harsh lights, gigantic menus, obsequious waiters, and Alan eyeing other women.

"You don't even know me," he said during one of his marathon phone calls in which he did all of the talking. "I did have a severe fear of closeness before, and as you noticed, I was only interested in things outside myself. I was afraid of being exposed as a fraud. I have always suspected myself of having nothing good or substantial inside. I didn't want it discovered so I *did* push you far away . . . I'm an expert at it. Suddenly other women become attractive to me . . . when I am in danger of caring deeply for someone . . . like you."

Oh, Alan, why are you telling me these boring things, we tried and it didn't work, we had nothing to talk about and you made me feel unattractive, I can't stand your taste in painting and literature, I hate your scarab pinky ring, carefully styled beard, gymnastic approach, I can't even allow anyone to bang me over the head with a flute

"I used to be very compulsive about women... used them to alleviate anxiety about myself."

It continued with orange carnations every other day and finally a flamelike flower called Celosia. The telephone calls became urgent and annoying.

"A long time ago I disconnected sex from my feelings, made it an abstract skill... you called it acrobatics. You were harsh but partly right. I *have* done the same or similar things with every woman I have known. No one ever objected before... I'm not even sure I know what else to do. I feel ridiculous. At my age I'm not sure what I would do with a woman... I guess I would have to ask... find out. I don't know if I can do that... somehow it disturbs me."

"Maybe you're worrying about it and analyzing it too much in the abstract... No, I don't want to go out to dinner. You know I never enjoyed dining out. There was too much pressure... Yes, I'll think about it."

Why would I want to have dinner with you, I would have to be completely out of my mind, you never paid any attention to me and we disliked everything about each other, you even objected to my height and to my paintings, those Celosia are like red flames

"I want to tell you what happened to me after I last saw you... I became impotent for the first time. I don't mean that it was your fault... I've stopped doing that. I have always felt insufficient as a man... despite the external things... my looks, credentials... the right schools... social status—things I once thought important, you know... assistant editor of *The Harvard Law Review*... maybe you don't understand how important these things are to some people. I was always very attractive to women... in part because of those credentials but that never bothered me. And I handle my law practice very well. Foreign banks consult me about loans... even other corporate lawyers call to discuss financial investments with me..."

"Maybe you could get to the point. I'm interested but my ear is starting to hurt... I know, but I'm not ready to dine out."

"The point is that my personal problems were well-concealed. Not like yours. Try not to become defensive but your behavior has been erratic—at least since I've known you. I needed to feel, to believe that there was nothing wrong with me, particularly as a man and that, unlike you and other people, I could solve all my problems myself. I considered anything else an admission of defeat. Am I boring you? I want you to understand.

"Remember how hostile I was to your painting? It was their direct feelings... feelings admitted... they made me nervous. I preferred to avoid any kind of self-realization. It's hard for a man to see his own problems... he feels weak and inadequate. I blamed the impotence on you... you had been castrating. I tried with one woman after another. It wouldn't work anymore... I could no longer successfully separate my body from my other feelings."

"Are you finished fucking the entire female universe?"

"Please don't get hostile and defensive... try to separate this from your own needs for a minute... that's a problem that you have to work on. Anyhow I tried to deny the whole problem and threw myself into sports—tennis, jogging, squash, basketball—like some foolish, aging jock. Finally I decided to get some help. That was so hard for me... it still is. But I wanted to be better than I was. I'm still the same in many ways... but... You know if we're ever together again I want you to have the very best of me."

—

I have finally said yes. Not simply because I am lonely but because he sends me flame-like flowers and because he returned after running away. No one ever has. Nor has any other man ever admitted that even some part of the problem was his. I respect him for that and I am also beginning to like his attempts at being honest with me. But I don't really trust him. He could run away again—or make me feel unattractive.

"Alan," I said, "I will have dinner with you if we can find a small, dimly lit restaurant, if I am not pressured to order foods you love and I find nauseating, and if you think you can pay some attention to me instead of staring at all the other beautiful women and flirting with the waitress. If you can't manage these things then I'd rather skip it."

There was a long silence during which my heart beat rapidly with anxiety about making the requests, and during which Alan must have been weighing the pros and cons.

"That's perfectly reasonable, Ellen. I will try to make you feel as comfortable as possible . . . but I might do something wrong anyhow, so if you don't expect everything to be perfect, I think we'll be fine. I'm struggling also . . . just try not to magnify my mistakes, please."

I was astonished—since when were any of my requests reasonable, not to mention "perfectly" so? Hadn't Adolphe left and not returned for days when I asked him if we could lie down together? Didn't George foam at the mouth and tear rags when I expressed an opinion that contradicted his own? And I remember that Rombert always refused when I asked him if he would sleep over on 72nd Street. All of them, in fact, had always done whatever they wished, sexually or otherwise, without taking my wishes into consideration at all. Melita's Peter thought it was his right to sneak into my bed when Melita was asleep. Plink assumed that I wanted to be hit over the head with his flute. Auriel considered it his right to possess me as well as a harem of other women whose nipples he painted with the identical sable brush.

Alan's response was an experience so new, so unique, and so unexpected that I became somewhat nervous about it. I worried that he was martyring himself and would make up for it later by slitting my throat or discovering some blemish on me. Or he might simply forget to put my requests into action when it came down to the real situation. Or else, once having achieved his goal of torturing me in a restaurant he would become satiated, stop sending flowers, and never call again.

—

We are in a small Cuban restaurant called Frini's. It is on Amsterdam Avenue between 72nd and 73rd Streets. It isn't bad really. At least it is small and there are only four other couples. On the walls are bulls' heads, bullfighters' hats, and bunches of purple wax grapes. The tablecloth is red and a small candle burns inside a net-covered globe.

"Order anything you want—as much or as little as you please," Alan says, handing me a menu which is delightfully small and comprehensible. His hand is shaking I notice, and I have to stifle an urge to giggle. He is trying too hard. He has even guessed somehow that I dislike the scarab ring and his pinky is bare. It is much lighter there where the ring usually covers the skin. If I laugh he might think I am making fun of him. Then the entire evening could be spoiled—I do not think that Alan is ready to laugh at himself.

"I like this restaurant," I say, realizing that he has selected it with my preferences in mind. If it were entirely left to him we would be somewhere larger and more opulent.

My comment has pleased him. He relaxes a little. Now he is studying the menu. I know he wants to urge me to order something disgusting like poached frogs' eggs but he refrains. (I have already seen Alan looking at the waitress's ass, but I am trying not to let it upset me, I am trying not to be perfectionistic—to regard it as simply a normal movement of the eye.)

He looks at me intently—it is I who become embarrassed by his gaze, lower my eyes and look to the right wall—at the triangular matador hats displayed there. A part of me wants to hide.

"I'll have shrimp with yellow rice and black beans."

He makes no condescending comment and no disappointed expression appears on his face.

Alan orders crab soup followed by fried eel, boiled octopus *à la* Frini, a side dish of frogtit sauce, and sautéed mussels.

"Actually I like being here... the candlelight is nice... who knows, I may get to like dining out."

Alan looks at me and caresses the net-covered glass with his hand.

His face is quite interesting. I observe it differently in the candlelight. His hair is black with some auburn and gray in it and it is receding. There is a lot of gray in his short beard making him look very distinguished. Lines cross his forehead and there are deeper ones on either side of his nose. These keep his face from looking too classically handsome. But he looks so worried and so serious. I wish he could laugh at himself.

"Being a lawyer has been a way to escape personal involvements. I can see that now... not that I don't like the law... I've told you how excited I am about international corporate law. But first it was a way to be certain of a secure life... materially."

He looks at me. Alan's eyes are bluish-gray. I am getting to like them although I feel more comfortable with brown eyes.

"I have nothing against law or security... you seem to think that people in the arts feel above other professions."

"Yes, I do get that feeling sometimes—as though you have been let in on some universal secret, something I could never comprehend. I feel left out of it."

"Do you realize how ridiculous that is?"

"I don't think so. I can only see things that are right in front of me," he says.

"My mother drank a lot," he says abruptly, while lighting a long brown cigarette. "I want *you* to know... I've never told anyone about it before. She used to wander off and sometimes my father... *we* didn't know where she was. I always feared she had left me for good. Then we'd find out that she was drying out in some hospital."

I wish he weren't so serious and I also wish he wasn't smoking a brown cigarette. His eyes are a very subtle shade of blue—not cold.

"I should stop smoking," he says seeing me glance at his cigarette. "I'm talking too much... about myself."

"That's all right... you've been talking too much over the telephone for weeks. I'm used to it." I start to laugh, but he just can't laugh at himself.

"Later things got better. She joined AA and got it under control. My father was weak. I don't like weak people. He never said anything when she left or when she came back. He didn't get angry and he didn't try to help. He just looked defeated and let things happen.

"It made me angry. I thought he should *do* something so she wouldn't go away anymore. I made up my mind that I would never be weak like him. I never had any respect for my father. Everyone walked all over him. He had his good Mayflower name and a lot of social connections and that was it... but he didn't *do* anything... went into the bank a few hours in the morning—shuffled some papers around and then came home."

"Can't you forgive anyone for their weaknesses?"

"I think so... they live in California... Sebastapol... I don't see much of them. Maybe I'll fly out this Christmas.

"It's always been hard for me to trust women... I've always loved them physically but it wasn't good enough. It was tearing me apart. I have to grow... for a long time I have stayed the same... maybe I'm like Dad in that way... but I want to grow... enough of that... do you want dessert? Now you don't *have* to order it. I promise I won't badger you."

This time I can't help laughing. He smiles.

"I'll just have coffee. You can relax... I don't feel pressured anymore. I actually like being here... with you."

Alan's eyes are a very warm blue color and the hairs on his chest are black and gray. He has a gentle voice.

"What worries me is that I don't think I'm a particularly interesting person. That's one of my main fears concerning you. You're so imaginative. I'm a very good lawyer but there's nothing particularly creative in what I do—it's mainly organizational. I don't know if I could be enough for you... I had the usual art history courses...

minimal requirements but my taste isn't very well developed—not that I have to tell you that."

This time he laughs.

"You worry too much... you're as bad as I am."

"Yet I do feel that in some way we complement each other. Maybe we can add to each other... what do you think?"

"It's possible. I really don't know if we complement each other or if we clash. It's too soon. Let's just not pretend something is there if it isn't."

"I don't want to pretend either. I don't know whether or not I have anything to give you... I know the kind of things you need... they're from inside, not just material. Giving material things is easy for me. I just have to find out how much of myself I can give. That is my greatest concern—that I would let someone really get to know me and she would find nothing inside me... she would be disappointed and I would be disgusted with myself."

If you could only do magic tricks, make doves appear on your arms or fingertips, if you could make the world light up like Auriel did when he touched me, covered me with silk, unwrapped me slowly, painted bubbles and daisies

"Try not to worry so much. I don't think you are empty inside, and I feel much closer to you because you've let me know some of your fears... my problem is that I've always been in love with magic and with beauty and wanted someone to erase the pain of everyday reality. Of course no one can... I never wanted to be an ordinary person. I don't know how to be loved in an ordinary way... or if I want that... the day-to-day ups and downs, insecurities, being taken for granted, being treated like everyone else... it's hard for me... at least it has been in the past, and in my trying to get away from it I've done things that you might not be able to accept, that you might not understand... but I don't want to have to hide things or deny them even to myself."

I am thinking of all those radiant nights with magical strangers—of the caresses, flutes, stars, and scented bathwater.

"I don't want to hear about those things yet... but I know I can become stronger in that way. I know that anything you have done had a deep purpose... maybe even you didn't realize it... You look so pretty tonight."

He reaches across the table and takes my hand. I want him to but something within me pulls away. It is like a curtain shutting him out. I used to fill my loneliness with radiance, with beauty, with rainbow sensuality. Blind in my radiance where no loneliness can be felt. Isn't that where I belong? I want to be thrown into the red of a watermelon—to be one with it and part of it. I want to be part of the sounds of trees and the vision of stars and of the moon, without differentiation, so I could become a rock or a planet or water or the air... like Auriel's white light. I want to stay a child forever.

He notices my hand pulling away but doesn't let it go. He keeps holding it gently.

"I am afraid somehow," I say, not understanding it.

What you, Alan, don't understand is that in the radiance *I* am the center of the universe. Around me everything flows the way I wish. I can change old men into kings, pain into golden pleasure, burnt grass into soft velvet, myself into a bird or a flower. Everything spins around and around—so many colors and sensations. Perhaps it is better than being loved. I am afraid of ordinary days, Alan.

We are in Alan's bed. Everything is calm and candlelit.

"You don't have to prove anything to me you know."

"I know... but it's a habit. This is like starting all over again. I have never felt this." He holds me close to him and kisses my face gently, even my eyelids.

Again I find myself pulling back.

Go away, I don't want you here, I don't want you coming so close to me, there are no painted flowers on my breasts, there are no drugged spiders on my thighs to hide me, where are my veils, I feel too naked, where are my gowns, my crown, where is my prince

"Don't turn away, please," he says softly.

"I can't do this. I can't."

He hears but he pushes inside me very slowly and holds me rocking back and forth. That is all. No turning upside down, no silver stars, nets, masks, or bubbles on my breasts. I am terrified. I am not even sure that I am breathing.

He stops moving and looks right into my eyes. I start to turn away and become cold. Gently he turns my head back holding my chin. He kisses my lips.

"We are going to be all right. You'll see. I love you very much."

—

Clear even light is falling on the tablecloth and on the gold-rimmed china cups. Alan holds me close to him for a moment before leaving.

"Paint well . . . you know what I mean . . . I adore you all day long . . . remember that."

It isn't as hard as I thought it would be, the day-to-day comings and goings. Sometimes the small desertions hurt for a while.

I close the door gently and fasten the latch. I brush the breadcrumbs off the tablecloth with my hands and begin to rinse the plates. I like the feel of the warm water and soap on the china.

I glance out the window of the Mayfair Towers down to where huge clumps of snow are slashed on one side with sunlight. The building across the street is also broken into dark and sunlit patterns. How clear it is. The sky above 72nd Street is one even blue. Auriel's cheeks are red and cold. I see him from above, from across the street, as he stands on his usual corner. He wears a sweater under his flowered shirt and a multicolored scarf around his neck. The doves are flecked with sunlight as they fly from nowhere and flutter onto the tips of his fingers. People watch wearing overcoats and boots and woolen gloves. I see their hands applaud as Auriel smiles faintly. I am far away in my new apartment with its hissing radiator, wicker basket of apples, and gold-rimmed china. But I continue to watch from inside as he gathers the money, as he replaces the doves carefully in their cage. A woman is holding Auriel's tapestried bag. She has long dark hair and tiny wrists. Auriel rolls a snowball and throws it at her feet. When it lands it disintegrates. I wipe a tear away. How clear the sky is. I have never seen the sun so bright.

ACKNOWLEDGMENTS

With thanks to the Corporation of Yaddo and to its wonderful staff. Without Yaddo's gracious hospitality, I would not have had the concentrated time for the completion of this work.

With thanks to my friend Rawn for her emotional support.

With appreciation to Writers For Our Time whose youthful and mature black writers have willingly opened their membership to share growth and to exchange ideas with their white sister and brother writers.

And with ever-growing admiration and loyalty to the fine writers of The Fiction Collective—the organization of diversely innovative writers of which I am proud to be a member.

e. k.

BREAKFAST AT TIFFANY'S

Truman Capote

'What I've found does the most good is just to get into a taxi and go to Tiffany's. It calms me down right away, the quietness and the proud look of it; nothing very bad could happen to you there, not with those kind men in their nice suits . . .'

It's New York in the 1940s, where the martinis flow from cocktail hour till breakfast at Tiffany's. And nice girls don't, except, of course, Holly Golightly. Pursued by Mafia gangsters and playboy millionaires, Holly is a fragile eyeful of tawny hair and turned-up nose, a heartbreaker, a perplexer, a traveller, a tease. She is irrepressibly 'top banana in the shock department', and one of the shining flowers of American fiction.

'One of the twentieth century's most gorgeously romantic fictions'
Daily Telegraph

MOON TIGER

Penelope Lively

Claudia Hampton, a beautiful, famous writer, lies dying in hospital. But, as the nurses tend to her with quiet condescension, she is plotting her greatest work: 'a history of the world ... and in the process, my own.' Gradually she recreates the rich mosaic of her life and times, conjuring up those she has known. There is Gordon, her adored brother, and Jasper, her charming, untrustworthy lover and father of Lisa, her cool, conventional daughter. Then there is Tom, her one great love, both found and lost in wartime Egypt. Penelope Lively's Booker Prize-winning novel weaves an exquisite mesh of memories, flashbacks and shifting voices, in a haunting story of loss and desire.

'Leaves its traces in the air long after you've put it away' Anne Tyler

QUARTET

Jean Rhys

With an Introduction by Katie Owen

Living in Paris with her reckless, vagabond husband Stephan, Marya is very near to being happy. She enjoys their haphazard existence, never questioning how he lives, never wanting to know the truth. When Stephan is suddenly imprisoned she is left penniless and alone. Taken up by a sophisticated English couple, the Heidlers, who gradually overwhelm her with their own desires, Marya finds her sense of reality slipping further and further away.

Set against a background of winter-wet streets and smoke-filled cafés, Jean Rhys's first novel is both poignant and disturbingly intimate in its vivid depiction of a woman on her own.

'She is loved for a special kind of courage' *Guardian*

GOOD MORNING, MIDNIGHT

Jean Rhys

In 1930s Paris, where one cheap hotel is very like another, a young woman is teaching herself indifference. She has escaped personal tragedy and has come to France to find courage and seek independence. She tells herself to expect nothing, especially not kindness, least of all from men. Tomorrow, she resolves, she will dye her hair blonde.

Jean Rhys was a talent before her time with an impressive ability to express the anguish of young, single women. In *Good Morning, Midnight*, Rhys created the powerfully modern portrait of Sophia Jansen, whose emancipation is far more painful and complicated than she could expect, but whose confession is flecked with triumph and elation.

'Her eloquence in the language of human sexual transaction is chilling, cynical and surprisingly moving' A. L. Kennedy

THE BALLAD OF THE SAD CAFÉ

Carson McCullers

Few writers have expressed loneliness, the need for human understanding and the search for love with such power and poetic sensibility as the American writer Carson McCullers.

In *The Ballad of the Sad Café*, a tale of unrequited love, Miss Amelia, a spirited, unconventional woman, runs a smalltown store and, except for a marriage that lasted just ten days, has always lived alone. Then Cousin Lymon appears from nowhere, a little, strutting hunchback who steals Miss Amelia's heart. Together they transform the store into a lively, popular café. But when her rejected husband Marvin Macy returns, the result is a bizarre love triangle that brings with it violence, hatred and betrayal.

Six stories by Carson McCullers also appear in this volume.

'Enchanting . . . an exquisite talent' *Sunday Times*

THE HEART IS A LONELY HUNTER

Carson McCullers

Carson McCullers' prodigious first novel was published to instant acclaim when she was just twenty-three. Set in a small town in the middle of the deep South, it is the story of John Singer, a lonely deaf-mute, and a disparate group of people who are drawn towards his kind, sympathetic nature. The owner of the café where Singer eats every day, a young girl desperate to grow up, an angry drunkard, a frustrated black doctor: each pours their heart out to Singer, their silent confidant, and he in turn changes their disenchanted lives in ways they could never imagine.

'I cannot think of any novel that I take more pleasure in re-reading'
Jonathan Bate

THE GREAT GATSBY

F. Scott Fitzgerald

'There was music from my neighbour's house through the summer nights. In his blue gardens men and girls came and went like moths among the whisperings and the champagne and the stars'

Day and night Jay Gatsby's mansion on West Egg buzzes with bright young things drinking, dancing and debating his mysterious character. For Gatsby – young, handsome, fabulously rich – always seems alone in the crowd, watching and waiting, although no one knows what for. Beneath the shimmering surface of his life he is hiding a secret longing that can never be fulfilled.

In *The Great Gatsby*, Fitzgerald brilliantly captures both the disillusion of post-war America and the moral failure of a society obsessed with wealth and status. But he does more than render the essence of a particular time and place, for in chronicling Gatsby's tragic pursuit of his dream, Fitzgerald recreates the universal conflict between illusion and reality.

'Not only a page-turner and a heartbreaker, it's one of the most quintessentially American novels ever written' *Time*

TENDER IS THE NIGHT

F. Scott Fitzgerald

'I don't ask you to love me always like this, but I ask you to remember. Somewhere inside me there'll always be the person I am tonight'

The French Riviera in the 1920s is 'discovered' by Dick and Nicole Diver, who turn it into the playground of the rich and glamorous. Among their circle is Rosemary Hoyt, the beautiful starlet, who falls in love with Dick and is enraptured by Nicole, unaware of the corruption and dark secrets that haunt their marriage. When Dick becomes entangled with Rosemary, he fractures the delicate structure of his relationship with Nicole, and the lustre of their life together begins to tarnish. *Tender is the Night* is an exquisite novel that reflects not only Fitzgerald's own personal tragedy, but also the shattered idealism of the society in which he lived.

'A tragedy backlit by beauty' *Daily Express*

MRS DALLOWAY

Virginia Woolf

'She had a perpetual sense, as she watched the taxi cabs, of being out, out, far out to sea and alone; she always had the feeling that it was very, very dangerous to live even one day'

On a June morning in 1923, Clarissa Dalloway, the glittering wife of a Member of Parliament, is preparing for a party she is giving that evening. As she walks through London, buying flowers, observing life, her thoughts are of the past and she remembers the time when she was as young as her own daughter Elizabeth, her romance with Peter Walsh, now recently returned from India; and the friends of her youth. Elsewhere in London Septimus Smith is being driven mad by shell shock. As the day draws to its end, his world and Clarissa's collide in unexpected ways.

'One of the most moving, revolutionary artworks of the twentieth century' Michael Cunningham